THE TORRENTS OF SPRING

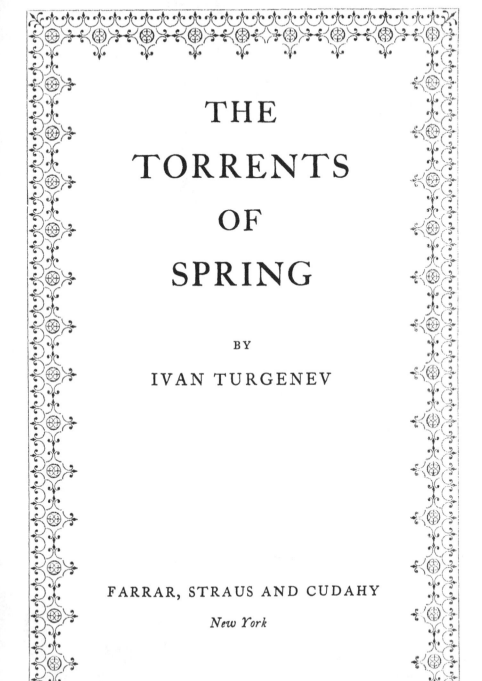

THE
TORRENTS
OF
SPRING

BY

IVAN TURGENEV

FARRAR, STRAUS AND CUDAHY

New York

ISBN: 0-37452-662-1

PRINTED IN GREAT BRITAIN BY
WESTERN PRINTING SERVICES LTD BRISTOL

*TRANSLATED FROM
THE RUSSIAN
BY*
DAVID
MAGARSHACK

———

Introduction

TURGENEV wrote *The Torrents of Spring* during the Franco-German war of 1870. He finished it six months after the capitulation of France. For most of that period—from November 1870 to February 1871—he lived in London, and this short novel, one of the greatest and least sentimental love stories in European literature, was most probably written there. Unlike any other novel by Turgenev, it is not the purely Russian political problems but the international crisis that left its mark on *The Torrents of Spring*. Indeed, the Franco-Prussian war brought about a change in Turgenev's hitherto violently pro-German sentiments. Turgenev never could forgive Germany for what he described as her 'aggressive rapacity' which, he predicted, would be 'the germ of new and more terrible wars'. It was no doubt under the influence of the political events of that time that in *The Torrents of Spring* Turgenev so scathingly satirized the German army officers, the German shop manager Klüber, the German man of letters P . . . , and the German theatre in Wiesbaden. This provoked a furious outcry in the Press in Germany as well as in the German Press in Russia. Turgenev refers to one of these attacks on him by a reviewer of the *St. Petersburg Zeitung* in a letter from Saint-Valéry-sur-Somme of 27 July 1872 to Ludwig Pietsch, the German artist and writer, who became one of his closest friends. 'Good heavens,' Turgenev wrote,

vii

'how touchy the Germans have become after their recent victories! What fastidious old maids! You can't bear the fact that in my last short novel I scratched you a little. But have I not dealt even greater blows at my own beloved countrymen? In the St. Petersburg (German) paper a critic has raised a hue and cry against me. He calls upon the officers of the German army to wipe the slanderer and insolent liar (that is, me!) off the face of the earth. Till now I credited the Germans with greater restraint and impartiality. I'm afraid I shall have to praise the Russians now, much as I dislike doing it. Do you really think that I berated that worthless Devrient and his miserable theatre *as a sop* to the French? My last novel may not be particularly good, but those few pinpricks are the best and most truthful things in it.'

But while the references to the Germans in the story are purely incidental, its main plot—Sanin's love affair with Gemma—is based on a similar event in Turgenev's own life. Turgenev, like Sanin, fell in love with a girl in Frankfort. He, too, was twenty-two at the time and was returning from a tour of Italy and Switzerland. In Frankfort he, again like Sanin, went into a confectioner's shop and there a beautiful girl, the daughter of the proprietress, rushed out from an inner room and implored him to save her brother who had fainted. But the girl was not an Italian but a Jewess, and she had a sister as well as a brother. Turgenev fell in love with her and it was only after a long inner struggle that he could bring himself to leave Frankfort.

Turgenev made the acquaintance of the prototype of the old Italian singer Pantaleone in the household of a Russian prince many years later.

Another more subtle and profound autobiographical element in the story concerns its hero's infatuation with the rich Russian woman, the daughter of a peasant, which is paralleled in Turgenev's own life by his infatuation with the famous singer Pauline Viardot, the daughter of a Spanish gipsy. This tragic element of love, an obsession leading to a man's ruin, so strikingly depicted in *The Torrents of Spring*, is, as might be expected, one of the constantly recurring themes in Turgenev's stories.

No less autobiographical is the introductory passage of the short novel in which Turgenev, who, like Sanin, was fifty-two at the time, gives such a vivid description of the fear of death that had haunted him for so many years and his feeling, magnified by the hostility aroused in Russia by his major works, of the utter futility of life.

Turgenev was, naturally perhaps, in view of the failure of his longer novels in Russia, not very optimistic about the success of *The Torrents of Spring*. In a letter to the Russian poet Yakov Polonsky on 18 December 1871, he wrote that he did not expect that his novel would be liked in Russia. 'It is a rather long love story,' he declared, 'which contains no hint of any social, political or contemporary events. If I am mistaken,' he concluded, 'all the better.' Turgenev, as it turned out, was mistaken. The novel was first published in 1871 in the January issue of the Moscow periodical *The European Herald*. It was an instantaneous success. The issue of the periodical had to be reprinted, an unprecedented event in the history of Russian periodicals. This unexpected success is, no doubt, to be ascribed chiefly to the uncontroversial nature of its plot. The absence of any contemporary elements in the novel coupled with the deeply felt personal experiences of its author which found expression in it also account for its unfailing impact on the non-Russian reader and is a pretty certain guarantee of its continuing popularity as a work of art. It was Gustave Flaubert who found the right words in which to express his admiration for Turgenev's masterpiece. 'Ah,' he wrote to Turgenev on 2 August 1873, 'this is a love story if ever there was one! You know everything there is to know about life and you know how to put it into words, which is an even rarer accomplishment. *Quel homme que mon ami Tourguéneff! Quel homme!'*

D.M.

Years of gladness,
Days of glee,
Like torrents of spring,
They flee, they flee!

From an old folk-song

A т two o'clock in the morning he returned to his study. He sent away his servant, who had lighted the candles, and, flinging himself into an armchair by the fireplace, buried his face in his hands.

Never before had he felt so exhausted—bodily and spiritually. He had spent a whole evening in the company of attractive women and cultured men; some of the women were beautiful, almost all the men were distinguished by intellect and talent; he himself had talked with great success and even brilliantly but, in spite of all that, he had never before been so overwhelmed by the *taedium vitae*, the 'disgust with life', of which the Romans had already spoken. He felt almost stifled by it. Had he been a little younger, he would have cried from sheer boredom, dejection and exasperation: a feeling of corrosive, burning bitterness, like the acrid taste of wormwood, filled his whole soul. Something inescapably hateful, something horribly wearisome encompassed him on all sides like a dark autumn night; and he did not know how to get rid of that darkness, that bitterness. He could not count on falling asleep: he knew he would not sleep.

He began thinking—slowly, listlessly, splenetically.

He thought of the vanity, the uselessness, the vulgar falsity of all things human. All the ages of man passed one by one before his mind's eye (he had himself turned fifty-two only recently) and he could find nothing good to say of any of them. Everywhere there was the same everlasting futility, the same ineptitude, the same kind of half-genuine, half-conscious self-delusion: anything for a quiet life! And then all of a sudden, like a bolt from the blue, old age comes upon you and with it the ever-growing, corroding and undermining fear of death and—down into the black abyss with you! And, of course, you are lucky if that is the way your life works out. For it is quite possible that before the end, like rust on iron, there will be sickness and suffering. . . . Life did not seem to him to be like a storm-tossed sea, as the poets describe it. No. He imagined that sea to be smooth and unruffled, calm as a millpond and transparent to its darkest bottom; he himself sat in a small, unsteady boat, and down below on that dark, slimy bottom he could just make out the shapes of hideous monsters, looking like huge fishes: all the maladies and infirmities of life—grief, madness, poverty, blindness. . . . Even while he looked, one of the monsters detached itself from the darkness, rose higher and higher, became more and more distinct, more and more horribly distinct. . . . Another moment and the boat that bore him would be overturned. But then it seemed to grow indistinct again, it withdrew further and further, it sank to the bottom, and there it lay stirring the water round it faintly. . . . But the appointed hour would come, and it would overturn the boat.

He shook his head, jumped up from the chair, took two turns round the room, sat down at the writing-table and, pulling out one drawer after another, began

xii

rummaging among his old letters, mostly from women. He did not know himself why he was doing it; he was not looking for anything in particular, he merely wanted to rid himself by some kind of external occupation of the thoughts that troubled him. Opening at random some of the letters (in one of them there was a withered flower tied round with a faded ribbon), he merely shrugged his shoulders and, casting a glance at the fireplace, he flung them aside, probably intending to burn all this useless rubbish. Hurriedly thrusting his hands first into one then into another drawer, he suddenly opened his eyes wide and, slowly pulling out a small hexagonal box of old-fashioned make, he slowly raised its lid. In the box, under two layers of cotton-wool, yellow with age, there was a little garnet cross.

For a few moments he gazed bewildered at this little cross, and suddenly he uttered a faint cry. . . . There was an expression of regret and at the same time of joy on his face. Such an expression appears on a man's face when he suddenly happens to meet someone he has long lost sight of, whom he has been very fond of in the past and who now appears unexpectedly before him, looking the same, and yet totally changed by the years.

He got up and, going back to the fireplace, sat down again in the armchair, and again buried his face in his hands. . . . 'Why today? Just today?' he thought and he remembered many things, many things of long ago. . . .

This is what he remembered. . . .

But first I should mention his name, his patronymic and his surname. He was called Dimitry Pavlovich Sanin.

This is what he remembered.

1

I<small>T</small> all happened in the summer of 1840. Sanin was twenty-two and he was in Frankfort on his way home from Italy to Russia. He was a man of independent means, though his fortune was not large, and he had almost no family ties. After the death of a distant relative, he was left a few thousand roubles and made up his mind to spend them abroad before joining the Civil Service, before, that is, finally assuming the government yoke without which he thought it impossible to achieve any security. Sanin carried out his plan exactly as he had conceived it and arranged things so skilfully that on the day of his arrival in Frankfort he had only just enough money left to enable him to return to Petersburg. In 1840 there were only very few railways in existence; tourists travelled by stage-coach. Sanin booked a seat in a *Beiwagen*; but the coach was not leaving until eleven o'clock at night. He had plenty of time left. Fortunately, the weather was excellent, and after having dinner at the White Swan, an hotel that was famous in those days, he went for a walk in the town. He went in to have a look at Dannecker's 'Ariadne', which he did not like very much, paid a visit to the house of Goethe, of whose works, however, he had read only *Werther*, and that in a French translation; he walked along the bank of the Main, was rather bored, as indeed any respectable traveller could be expected to be; at last, at six o'clock in the evening, tired and with dusty boots, he found himself in one of the least important streets in Frankfort. That street he could not forget for a long, long time afterwards. On one of its few houses he saw a signboard: 'Italian Confectionery, Giovanni Roselli', it announced to passers-by. Sanin went in to have a glass of lemonade; but in the first room where, behind a modest counter, on the shelves of a painted cupboard, recalling a chemist's shop, stood several bottles with gold labels and as many glass jars of biscuits, chocolates, and acid drops—in that room there was not a living soul; only a grey cat closed and opened its eyes and purred as it played with its paws on a tall wicker chair by the window, and a large ball of red wool, glowing brightly in the slanting rays of the evening sun, lay on the floor next to an overturned carved wooden workbox. There was a confused noise in the next room. Sanin stood still for a little while and, after waiting for the doorbell to stop ringing, raised his voice and said, 'Is there no one here?' At that moment the door of the next room opened and—Sanin could not help being astonished.

2

A GIRL of nineteen, her dark tresses falling over her
bare shoulders and her bare arms stretched out in front
of her, ran wildly into the shop and, seeing Sanin, at
once rushed up to him, seized him by the arm and
pulled him after her, saying in a breathless voice:
'Quick, quick! This way! Save him!' Sanin did not
follow the girl immediately, not because he did not
wish to answer her appeal, but simply because he was
too surprised to do anything. He seemed to be rooted
to the spot: never in his life had he seen such a beautiful girl. She turned to him and exclaimed 'Come,
please, come!' with such despair in her voice, in her
eyes and in the gesture of her clenched fist which she
put up spasmodically to her pale cheek, that he at once
rushed after her through the open door.

In the room into which he had run after the girl, on
an old-fashioned horsehair sofa, lay a boy of fourteen,
looking very white—white with a yellowish tinge, like
wax or old marble. He was quite amazingly like the
girl, evidently her brother. His eyes were closed, the
shadow of his thick black hair fell like a stain on his
forehead, which seemed to have been turned to stone,
and on his delicate, unruffled eyebrows; between the
lips, which had gone blue, could be seen clenched

3

teeth. He did not seem to be breathing. One of his hands had fallen to the floor and the other was thrown back over his head. The boy was dressed and his coat was buttoned up; a necktie was tied tightly round his neck.

The girl rushed wailing up to him.

'He's dead! He's dead!' she cried. 'A moment ago he was sitting here and talking to me and all of a sudden he collapsed and lay without moving. . . . Oh dear, can nothing be done to help him? And Mother is out, too! Pantaleone, Pantaleone, what about the doctor?' she added suddenly in Italian. 'Have you been to fetch him?'

'Signorina, I have not, I sent Louise,' someone said in a hoarse voice behind the door, and a little bandy-legged old man came limping into the room. He wore a lavender frock-coat with black buttons, a high white cravat, nankeen breeches and blue woollen stockings. His tiny face disappeared completely under a great mass of iron-grey hair. Rising sharply on every side and falling back in unkempt tufts, it made him resemble a ruffled hen, a resemblance all the more striking since under the dark grey mass one could only just make out a beak-like nose and a pair of round yellow eyes.

'Louise will run faster than I, and I can't run,' the old man went on in Italian, dragging his flat, gouty feet on which he wore high-laced boots. 'I've brought some water.'

He clasped the long neck of a bottle with his wasted crooked fingers.

'But Emilio will die in the meantime!' cried the girl, stretching out her hands to Sanin. 'Oh, sir, *mein Herr*, can't you help him?'

'He ought to be bled,' observed the old man called Pantaleone. 'He's had a stroke.'

4

Though Sanin had not the faintest idea about medicine, he did know that fourteen-year-old boys do not have strokes.

'It's a fainting fit, not a stroke,' he said, addressing Pantaleone. 'Have you any brushes?'

'What?' the old man asked, lifting his tiny face.

'Brushes, brushes,' Sanin repeated in German and French. 'A brush,' he added, making as if to brush his coat.

The old man understood him at last.

'Oh, brushes! *Spazzette!* Of course we've got brushes!'

'Let's have them. We'll take off his coat and give him a rub down.'

'Good. . . . *Benone!* And shouldn't we pour water on his head?'

'No. . . . Later. Go and fetch the brushes now, and be as quick as you can.'

Pantaleone put the bottle on the floor, rushed out and returned at once with two brushes, one a hairbrush and the other a clothes-brush. A curly poodle accompanied him and, wagging his tail vigorously, gazed inquisitively at the old man, the girl and even Sanin, as though wishing to find out what had caused all the commotion.

Sanin quickly took off the boy's coat, loosened his collar, rolled up his shirt sleeves and, arming himself with a brush, began rubbing his chest and arms with all his might. Pantaleone rubbed away with equal zest at his boots and trousers with the other—the hairbrush. The girl flung herself on her knees beside the sofa and, clutching her head with both hands, gazed intently and without blinking at her brother's face.

Sanin rubbed away and—kept stealing glances at her. Good Lord, how beautiful she was!

3

HER nose was rather large, but of a beautiful aquiline shape; her upper lip was lightly touched with down; her complexion was smooth and of a lovely mat texture, looking exactly like ivory or milky amber; her hair had a wavy sheen, like that of Allorio's Judith in the Palazzo Pitti; and most of all her eyes, dark grey with a black rim round the pupils, magnificent, triumphant eyes—even now when fear and grief clouded their brilliance. . . . Sanin could not help recalling the wonderful country from which he had just returned. . . . Why, even in Italy he had not come across anything like that! The girl breathed slowly and unevenly; it seemed as though she were waiting every time to see whether her brother would start breathing.

Sanin went on massaging him; but he looked not only at the girl. Pantaleone's queer figure also attracted his attention. The old man was utterly exhausted and out of breath; at every stroke of the brush, he jumped up and down and groaned loudly, while his huge mane of hair, moist with perspiration, swayed heavily to and fro, as though it were the roots of some large plant, washed loose by water.

'Won't you at least take his boots off?' Sanin was about to say to him.

6

The poodle, probably excited by the unusual nature of what was going on around him, suddenly sank on its front paws and started barking.

'*Tartaglia—canaglia!*' the old man hissed at him.

But at that moment the girl's face was transformed. Her eyebrows rose and her eyes grew larger and shone with joy.

Sanin looked round. . . . The young boy's face had become suffused with colour, his eyelids stirred, his nostrils quivered. He drew in the air through his still clenched teeth and sighed.

'Emilio!' cried the girl. '*Emilio mio!*'

The boy's large black eyes opened slowly. They still had a dazed look, but already they were smiling—faintly; the same faint smile hovered over his pale lips. Then he moved his drooping hand and flung it on his chest.

'*Emilio!*' repeated the girl and sat up. The expression of her face was so intense and vivid that it seemed that any moment she might burst into tears or laughter.

'Emilio! What's the matter? Emilio!' someone cried behind the door, and a neatly dressed woman with silvery grey hair and a dark face came quickly into the room. An elderly man walked in after her; the maid's head could be seen over his shoulders.

The girl ran to meet them.

'He's saved, Mother, he's alive!' she cried, impulsively embracing the lady who had just come in.

'But what's the matter?' she repeated. 'I come back and all of a sudden I meet the doctor and Louise.'

The girl started telling them what had happened, while the doctor went up to the patient, who was recovering more and more, and went on smiling; he seemed to be ashamed of the alarm he had caused.

'I see you've been massaging him with brushes,' the

7

doctor said to Sanin and Pantaleone, 'that was good—an excellent idea. . . . And now let's see if there's anything else we can do.' He felt the young man's pulse. 'Hm! Show me your tongue!'

The woman bent over him solicitously. He smiled still more frankly, raised his eyes to her and blushed . . .

It occurred to Sanin that he was no longer wanted and he went out into the shop. But before he had time to take hold of the handle of the street-door, the girl appeared before him again and stopped him.

'You're going?' she began, looking affectionately at his face. 'I won't keep you, but you must come to see us this evening. We owe you so much—you probably saved my brother's life and we want to thank you—my mother wants to. You must tell us who you are, you must celebrate with us. . . .'

'But,' Sanin said hesitantly, 'I'm leaving for Berlin today.'

'You've plenty of time,' the girl replied quickly. 'Please come back in an hour for a cup of chocolate. Promise? I'm afraid I must go back to him now. You'll come, won't you?'

What could Sanin do?

'I will,' he replied.

The beautiful girl pressed his hand rapidly and was gone; and he found himself in the street.

4

WHEN, an hour and a half later, Sanin returned to the Roselli confectionery shop, he was received like one of the family. Emilio was sitting on the same sofa on which he had been massaged, the doctor had given him a prescription and advised him to avoid any undue excitement, for his young patient was highly strung and predisposed towards heart disease. He had had fainting fits before, but never before had his fit lasted so long or been so violent. However, the doctor had said that the boy was out of danger. Emilio, as befitted a convalescent, was dressed in a large, comfortable dressing-gown; his mother had wrapped a blue woollen scarf round his neck; but he looked cheerful, almost gay; and, indeed, everything around looked gay. A huge porcelain coffee-pot filled with fragrant chocolate stood on a round table before the sofa; the table was covered with a clean cloth and round the coffee-pot were cups, decanters of soft drinks, biscuits, rolls and even flowers; six slender wax candles were burning in two antique silver candlesticks; a soft Voltaire chair was placed invitingly on one side of the sofa and Sanin was made to sit down in it. All the inhabitants of the confectionery shop he had happened to become acquainted with on that day were there to welcome

9

him, not excluding the poodle Tartaglia and the cat; everyone seemed to be indescribably happy; the poodle even sneezed with pleasure; only the cat kept screwing up its eyes and mincing as before. They made Sanin tell them who he was, where he came from and what his name was; when he said he was a Russian, the two ladies were a little surprised and even uttered little cries, and at once declared in one voice that his German accent was perfect, but that if he found it more convenient to speak French, he could use that language also, for both of them understood and spoke it well. Sanin at once availed himself of their suggestion. 'Sanin? Sanin!' The two ladies had not expected a Russian surname to be so easy to pronounce. His Christian name 'Dimitry' they liked very much too. The elder lady observed that when she was a young girl she had heard a beautiful opera 'Demetrio e Polibio', but that 'Dimitry' was much nicer than 'Demetrio'. In this way Sanin talked for about an hour. For their part, the ladies initiated him into all the details of their own life. The mother, the white-haired lady, did most of the talking. Sanin learnt from her that her name was Leonora Roselli, that she was a widow and that her late husband, Giovanni Battista Roselli, had settled in Frankfort twenty-five years before as a pastrycook; that Giovanni Battista had come from Vicenza and was a very good man, though a rather quick-tempered and haughty person, and a republican into the bargain! Saying this, Signora Roselli pointed to his portrait, painted in oils, and hanging over the sofa. It must be supposed that the artist, 'also a republican!' as Signora Roselli observed with a sigh, had not quite succeeded in catching a likeness, for in his portrait the late Giovanni Battista appeared as a gloomy and stern-faced brigand—something like Rinaldo

Rinaldini! Signora Roselli herself was a native of 'the ancient and beautiful city of Parma, where you can see the wonderful dome painted by the immortal Correggio!' But because of her long sojourn in Germany she had become almost a German herself. Then she added with a mournful shake of her head that all she had left in the world was *this* daughter and *this* son (she pointed to each in turn), that the daughter's name was Gemma and the son's Emilio, that they were both very good and obedient children, especially Emilio ('Am I not obedient?' her daughter objected, but her mother replied, 'Oh, you are a republican too!'); that her business affairs were of course in a worse state than they had been when her husband was alive, for he was an expert at the pastrycook's art ('*Un grand' uomo!*' Pantaleone put in sternly); but that, thank God, they could still make a living!

5

GEMMA listened to her mother, laughing softly to herself, or sighing, or stroking her shoulder or shaking a finger at her, or glancing at Sanin; at last she got up, embraced her mother and kissed her in the hollow of her neck, which made her mother laugh and even squeal a little. Pantaleone was also introduced to Sanin. It appeared that he had once been an opera singer, a baritone, but had long since given up his theatrical work, and that his position in the Roselli family was something between a friend of the family and a servant. In spite of his rather long stay in Germany, his German was execrable, and he knew only how to swear in it, mercilessly mispronouncing even the swear-words. '*Verroffukto spiccebubbio!*' was what he called almost every German. His Italian accent, on the other hand, was perfect, for he was a native of Sinigaglia, where one can hear '*lingua toscana in bocca romana!*' Emilio was quite unashamedly luxuriating and giving himself up to the pleasant sensations of one who has only just escaped a danger or is recovering from an illness; and, besides, it was abundantly clear that his family spoiled him. He thanked Sanin shyly, but preferred to give all his attention to the sweets and the soft drinks. Sanin was forced to drink two large cups of excellent chocolate and eat quite an extraordinary number of cakes; as soon as he had swallowed one, Gemma offered him another—and it was quite impossible to refuse! He soon felt at home: time flew with incredible swiftness. He had to tell them a lot of things—about Russia in general, the Russian climate, Russian society, the Russian peasant—and especially about the Cossacks; about the 1812 campaign, Peter the Great, the Kremlin and the Russian songs and church-bells. The two ladies had a very hazy idea of our vast and remote motherland; Signora Roselli or Frau Lenore, as she was more often called, even astonished Sanin by asking whether the famous ice-palace, built in the last century, still existed in Petersburg. She had read such an interesting article about it in one of her late husband's books: *Bellezze delle arti*. And in reply to Sanin's exclamation: 'Do you really think there is never any summer in Russia?' Frau Lenore replied that till then she had always imagined Russia to be like this: eternal snow, everyone walking about in fur coats, and every man a soldier, but that the people were extremely hospitable and all the peasants very docile. Sanin did his best to give her and her daughter more exact information. When the conversation touched on Russian music he was at once asked to sing some Russian airs, and they pointed to a tiny piano in the room with black keys instead of white and white instead of black. He obeyed without raising any objections and, accompanying himself with two fingers of his right and three fingers (the thumb, middle and little one) of his left hand, he sang in a thin nasal tenor first *Sarafan*, then *Along the Highroad*. The ladies praised his voice and the music, but were even more impressed by the softness and sonorousness of the Russian language, and asked for a translation of the text. Sanin did as they asked, but as the words of *Sarafan* and especially of *Along the Highroad (Sur une rue pavée une jeune fille allait à l'eau* was how he rendered the meaning of the original) could not give his listeners a high opinion of Russian poetry, he first recited, then translated, and then sang Pushkin's *I Remember a Wonderful Moment*, set to music by Glinka, whose minor bars he skipped over a little. But the ladies were in raptures over it, Frau Lenore even discovering quite a striking similarity between Russian and Italian. *Mgnoveniye* (a moment) —*o vieni, so mnoy* (with me) —*siam noi*, and so on. Even the names of Pushkin (which she pronounced Pussekin) and Glinka sounded like her native tongue to her. Sanin, for his part, asked the ladies to sing something: they did not stand on ceremony, either. Frau Lenore sat

13

down at the piano and sang with Gemma a few duets and *stornelle*. The mother once had a good contralto voice; the daughter's voice was rather weak, but pleasant.

BUT it was not Gemma's voice, it was Gemma herself that Sanin was admiring. He was sitting a little behind and on one side of her and he thought that no palm tree—even in the poems of Benediktov, a poet in fashion at that time—could vie with the exquisite gracefulness of her figure. And when, at the tender notes, she turned her eyes upwards, he felt that no heaven could fail to open up at such a look. Even old Pantaleone who, his shoulder leaning against the side of the door and his chin and mouth tucked into his ample cravat, was listening solemnly with the air of a connoisseur—even he could not take his eyes off the girl's lovely face and marvelled at it, and yet he of all people should have got used to it! Having finished the last duet with her daughter, Frau Lenore remarked that Emilio had an excellent voice, pure silver, but that he had now reached the age when the voice broke (he really did talk in a kind of bass that was constantly breaking) and that was why he was forbidden to sing; but that Pantaleone could, in honour of their guest, show what a fine singer he had been in his younger days. Pantaleone at once assumed a dissatisfied air, frowned, ruffled his hair, and declared that he had given it all up long ago, though he could certainly give a good account of himself when he was young, and that, as a matter of fact, he belonged to the great period of real classical singers—the present-day squealing performers were no match for them!—and a real school of singing; that he, Pantaleone Cippatola of Varese, had once been presented with a laurel wreath at Modena and that in honour of that occasion a number of white doves were released in the theatre; that, among others, a Russian Prince Tarbussky—*il principe Tarbussky*—with whom he had been on most friendly terms, had at dinner always invited him to go to Russia, promising him mountains of gold, mountains! —but that he could not bring himself to leave Italy, the land of Dante—*il paese del Dante!* Later on, of course, came—er—all sorts of misfortunes—he had not been discreet. . . . At this point the old man broke off, sighed deeply twice, dropped his eyes and began again talking of the classical period of singing, of the famous tenor Garcia, for whom he felt a deep, boundless reverence.

'That was a man!' he exclaimed. 'The great Garcia —*il gran Garcia*—never demeaned himself by singing falsetto like the contemptible tenors of today—*tenoracci*—always from the chest, the chest—*voce di petto, si!*' The old man gave a few violent taps with his little withered fist on his *jabot*. 'And what an actor! A volcano, *signori miei*, a volcano, *un Vesuvio!* I had the honour and the happiness of singing with him in the opera *dell' illustrissimo maestro* Rossini—in *Otello!*

Garcia was Otello, I was Iago—and when he uttered
the phrase . . .'

Here Pantaleone struck a pose and began to sing in
a trembling and hoarse, but still moving voice:

*'L'i . . . ra davver . . . so davver . . . so il fato
Io più no . . . no . . . no non temerò!*

The theatre shook, *signori miei*, but I did not lag
behind—I, too, sang after him:

*L'i . . . ra davver . . . so davver . . . so il fato
Temèr più non dovro!*

And suddenly, like lightning, like a tiger, he replied:
Morro! . . . ma vendicato. . . . And again, when he was
singing—when he was singing the famous aria from
Matrimonio segreto: Pria che spunti . . . then he, *il gran
Garcia,* after the words: *I cavalli di galoppo* at the
words: *Senza posa cacciera*—listen, how stupendous
it was, *com'è stupendo!* Here he made . . .' The old man
began some unusual *fioritura,* and, his voice breaking
on the tenth note, began to cough, and with a wave of
his hand, turned away murmuring: 'Why do you tor-
ment me?'

Gemma jumped up at once from her chair, and
clapping loudly and crying: Bravo! Bravo! rushed up
to the poor ex-Iago and patted him affectionately on
the shoulders with both hands. Emilio alone laughed
pitilessly. *Cet âge est sans pitié*—that age knows no
pity—La Fontaine has said that already.

Sanin tried to comfort the aged singer and began
talking to him in Italian (he had picked up a little
Italian during his last journey there) about *paese del
Dante, dove il si suona.* This phrase, together with
Lasciate ogni speranza, comprised the entire poetic lug-
gage of the young tourist; but Pantaleone resisted his

blandishments. Tucking his chin deeper than ever into his cravat and staring gloomily, he again looked like a bird, an angry bird at that—a raven or a black kite. It was then that Emilio, his face suddenly colouring slightly, which usually happens with spoilt children, turned to his sister and told her that if she wanted to entertain their guest, she could not do anything better than read him one of those short comedies of Malz which she read so well. Gemma laughed, slapped her brother on the hand, exclaiming, 'The things he thinks of!' She went at once to her room, however, and, returning with a small book in her hand, sat down at the table before the lamp, looked round, raised a finger: 'Silence, please!'—a typically Italian gesture— and began to read.

7

MALZ was a Frankfort writer who in the thirties wrote a number of very short, light comedies in the local dialect, in which he depicted local Frankfort types with ready and entertaining, though not very profound, humour. Gemma, it seemed, did read excellently, just like an actress. She brought out the peculiarities of every character and kept it up perfectly with the aid of mimicry she had inherited with her Italian blood; sparing neither her soft voice nor her beautiful face, she pulled most amusing faces when she had to represent some old woman in her dotage or a stupid mayor, screwing up her eyes, wrinkling her nose, squeaking, pronouncing her 'r's' in a guttural way. . . . During the reading she never laughed herself, but when her audience (with the exception, it is true, of Pantaleone, who left the room with indignation as soon as *quel verroflucto Tedesco* was mentioned), when her audience interrupted her by a burst of loud laughter, she put her book down on her knee and laughed loudly herself, tossing back her head, her black curls jumping in soft ringlets on her neck and her shaking shoulders. When the laughter stopped, she picked up her book at once, and again assuming the expression appropriate to the role she was acting, resumed her reading seriously. Sanin was full of admiration for her; he was particularly struck by the marvellous way in which her face, which was so ideally beautiful, quite miraculously assumed all at once such comic and sometimes almost trite expressions. The parts of young girls, the so-called *jeunes premières*, Gemma read less satisfactorily; with love scenes, in particular, she was least successful; she was aware of it herself and for that reason imparted a light shade of ridicule to them, as though she did not believe in all the rapturous vows and high-flown protestations, which the author himself, however, tried to refrain from as much as possible.

Sanin did not notice how quickly the evening had passed and he only remembered his imminent journey when the clock struck ten. He leapt up from his chair as if he had been stung.

'What's the matter?' asked Frau Lenore.

'Why, I should have left for Berlin today—I have booked a seat on the coach.'

'And when is the coach due to leave?'

'At half-past ten.'

'Well, in that case you won't be in time,' observed Gemma. 'Please, stay—I'll read you some more.'

'Have you paid for your ticket or only given a deposit?' Frau Lenore was curious to find out.

'I've paid for it,' Sanin cried plaintively with a sad grimace.

Gemma looked at him quizzically and—burst out laughing, but her mother scolded her.

'The young man has lost his money and you laugh!'

'Never mind,' replied Gemma, 'it won't ruin him, and we'll do our best to comfort him. Would you like some lemonade?'

Sanin drank a glass of lemonade, Gemma resumed her reading of Malz, and everything went, as before, swimmingly.

The clock struck twelve. Sanin got up to take his leave.

'You must stay in Frankfort for a few more days now,' said Gemma. 'Why be in a hurry? You won't have a better time in any other town.' She paused. 'I'm sure you won't,' she added, and smiled.

Sanin made no answer, thinking that as his purse was empty he would have to stay in Frankfort in any case until he received a reply from a friend in Berlin, whom he had intended to ask for some money.

'Please, please stay,' Frau Lenore said too. 'We'll introduce you to Gemma's fiancé, Herr Karl Klüber. He could not come today because he was very busy in his shop. I expect you must have seen a big draper's shop in the Zeile. Well, he's the manager there. But I'm sure he'll be very glad to call on you.'

19

Sanin—goodness only knows why—was rather taken aback by this piece of news. 'A lucky chap, that fiancé!' flashed across his mind. He looked at Gemma, and thought he noticed a mocking look in her eyes. He began saying goodbye.

'Till tomorrow? It is tomorrow, isn't it?' asked Frau Lenore.

'Till tomorrow!' declared Gemma in an affirmative and not interrogative tone of voice, as though it could not be otherwise.

'Yes, till tomorrow!' replied Sanin.

Emilio, Pantaleone and the poodle Tartaglia saw him off to the corner of the street. Pantaleone could not resist expressing his displeasure at Gemma's reading.

'She ought to be ashamed of herself! Pulling faces, squeaking—*una caricatura*! She should be acting the parts of Merope or Clytemnestra—something great, tragic, and she's taking off some disgusting German woman! Even I could do that. *Merz, kerz, schmerz!*' he added in a hoarse voice, thrusting out his face and spreading out his fingers.

Tartaglia barked at him and Emilio burst out laughing. The old man turned back sharply.

Sanin returned to the White Swan (he had left his things there in the public room) in a rather confused frame of mind. All those German-French-Italian conversations kept ringing in his ears.

'She's engaged!' he whispered, as he lay in bed in his modest hotel room. 'And what a beauty! But why did I stay?'

Next day, though, he sent a letter to his friend in Berlin.

8

HE had scarcely time to finish dressing when the waiter announced the arrival of two gentlemen. One of them was Emilio; the other, a tall, good-looking young man, was Herr Karl Klüber, the fiancé of the beautiful Gemma.

There can be little doubt that in the whole of Frankfort at that time there was not a more polite, decorous, dignified, amiable shop manager than Herr Klüber. His impeccable get-up was on the same level as the dignity of his carriage and the exquisiteness—a little reserved, and stiff, it is true, in the English style (he had spent two years in England) but still quite fascinating—exquisiteness of his manners! It was clear at the first glance that this handsome, somewhat severe, perfectly brought-up and excellently washed young man was accustomed to obey his superiors and issue orders to his inferiors and that behind the counter of his shop he must needs inspire respect even in his customers! There could be no doubt whatever about his quite abnormal honesty: one had only to look at his stiffly starched collar! And his voice, too, was what one would expect: deep, fruitily self-confident, but not too loud, even with a caressing note in its timbre. In such a voice it is particularly fitting to give orders to the shop assistants under one's control. 'Kindly show the lady that piece of crimson Lyons velvet!' or 'Please, let the lady have that chair!'

Herr Klüber began by introducing himself, bowing in such a dignified manner, drawing his feet together so agreeably and clicking his heels so courteously that one could not help but feel: 'That man's linen and moral qualities must be of the first order!' The finish of his bare right hand (in his left, invested in a suède glove, he held a hat shining like a looking-glass, with his other glove inside it)—the finish of the right hand, which he had held out modestly, but firmly, to Sanin, surpassed all belief: each finger-nail was perfection itself! Then he went on to explain in the choicest German that he wished to express his respect and his gratitude to the foreign gentleman who had rendered such a great service to his future relative, the brother of his fiancée; as he said this, he pointed with his left hand, in which he held his hat, to Emilio, who looked ashamed and, turning away to the window, put his finger in his mouth. Herr Klüber added that for his part he would be only too happy to be of some service to the foreign gentleman. Sanin replied, not without some difficulty, also in German, that he was very glad, that the service was not very great, and he asked his visitors to be seated. Herr Klüber thanked him and at once, spreading his coat tails, sank into a chair, but so lightly did he sink into it and so precariously did he sit on it that one could not help realizing that he had sat down out of politeness and would jump to his feet at any moment! And, indeed, he did jump up immediately and, shuffling his feet a couple of times uneasily, just as if he were dancing, he declared that he was sorry he could not stay any longer, for he had to hurry back to his shop—business before everything!

But as the next day was Sunday he had, with the consent of Frau Lenore and Fräulein Gemma, arranged an outing to Soden, to which he had the honour of inviting the foreign gentleman and he hoped that he would not refuse to grace it with his presence. Sanin did not refuse to grace it, and Herr Klüber bowed a second time and went out, his trousers of the most delicate shade of pea-green flashing agreeably and the soles of his brand-new boots squeaking no less agreeably.

9

EMILIO, who had remained standing with his face to the window even after Sanin's invitation to sit down, made a left-about turn as soon as his future relative had gone out and, pouting like a child and blushing, asked Sanin's permission to stay with him a little longer. 'I'm much better today,' he added, 'but the doctor has forbidden me to do any work.'

'Do stay, you're not interfering with me in the least,' exclaimed Sanin who, like every true Russian, was glad of any excuse for not doing any work himself.

Emilio thanked him, and in the shortest possible time

was quite at home with him and with his room; he examined his things and asked questions about almost every one of them: where he had bought it and what was its value. He helped him to shave, declaring that it was a pity he did not grow a moustache; finally, he told him a lot of things about his mother, his sister, Pantaleone and even the poodle Tartaglia, about how they lived and what they did. All traces of shyness disappeared in Emilio; suddenly he felt greatly attracted to Sanin, and not at all because Sanin had saved his life the day before, but because he was such a nice person! He did not lose time in letting Sanin into all his secrets. He insisted with special warmth that his mother had set her heart on his becoming a shopkeeper, while he *knew*, knew for certain, that he was born an artist, a musician, a singer, and that the theatre was his true vocation; that even Pantaleone encouraged him, but that HerrKlüber was on the side of his mother, over whom he had a great influence; that the very idea of making a shopkeeper of him was really Klüber's, for in his view nothing in the world could compare with the social position of a shopkeeper! To sell velvet and cotton and cheat the public, charging *Narren oder Russen-Preise* (fools' or Russian prices)—that was his ideal!

'Well,' he exclaimed, as soon as Sanin had finished dressing and written his letter to Berlin, 'now you must come and see us!'

'It's too early,' observed Sanin.

'That doesn't matter,' said Emilio, cajolingly. 'Let's go! We'll go to the post office and from there to our place. Gemma will be so glad to see you! You must have lunch with us. . . . You might put in a word to Mother about me and my career. . . .'

'All right, let's go!' said Sanin, and they set off.

10

GEMMA was most certainly pleased to see him and
Frau Lenore gave him a very friendly welcome too: it
was quite clear that he had made a good impression on
both of them the day before. Emilio ran out to see
about lunch, having first whispered in Sanin's ear:
'Don't forget!'

'I won't forget,' replied Sanin.

Frau Lenore was not feeling well: she had an attack
of migraine and, half-reclining in an armchair, tried
not to move about. Gemma wore a full yellow blouse
with a black leather belt round her waist; she, too,
looked tired and a little pale; there were dark rings
round her eyes, but they did not dim their brilliance,
and her pallor added a touch of charm and mystery to
the severe classical lines of her face. Sanin was particularly struck that day by the exquisite beauty of her
hands; when she smoothed or put back her dark shiny
curls with them, he could not take his eyes off her long
supple fingers, separated from each other like those of
Raphael's Fornarina.

It was very hot outside; after lunch Sanin was about
to take his leave, but they told him that on a day like
that it was best to stay in—and he agreed; he stayed. In
the back room, where he was sitting with his two

25

hostesses, it was very cool; the windows looked out upon a small garden overgrown with acacias. A great number of bees, wasps and bumble-bees were buzzing eagerly and without ceasing in their thick branches which were covered with golden blossoms; through the half-closed shutters and lowered blinds this continuous hum found its way into the room: it told of sultry heat in the open air—and the coolness of the shuttered, cosy house became all the sweeter.

Sanin talked a great deal, as on the day before, but not of Russia and not of Russian life. Wishing to please his young friend, who had been sent off to Herr Klüber's to practise book-keeping as soon as lunch was over, he began to talk about the comparative advantages and disadvantages of art and commerce. He was not surprised to learn that Frau Lenore was on the side of commerce—he had expected it; but Gemma, too, shared her views.

'If you're an artist, and especially a singer,' she maintained, with a vigorous downward movement of her hand, 'you must be able to get to the top. Second place is no good at all and who can tell whether you'll be able to get to the top?'

Pantaleone, who also took part in the conversation (as an old man and a servant of many years he was even allowed to sit in the presence of his masters; Italians in general are not very strict about etiquette), Pantaleone, of course, was all in favour of art. True, his arguments were rather weak; he spoke mostly of the necessity above all of possessing *un certo estro d'inspirazione*—a certain upsurge of inspiration! Frau Lenore remarked to him that he, too, of course, had possessed that *estro*, and yet...

'I had enemies,' Pantaleone observed darkly.

'But how do you know that Emilio would not have enemies even if this *estro* were discovered in him?'

26

'Well, make a tradesman of him,' Pantaleone said with vexation. 'Giovanni Battista would never have done it, though he was a pastrycook himself!'

'Giovanni Battista, my husband, was a sensible man —and if as a young man he was carried away by his enthusiasm——'

But the old man did not wish to hear anything more and left the room, muttering again reproachfully, 'Ah, Giovann' Battista!'

Gemma exclaimed that if Emilio had been a patriot and had wished to devote all his powers to the liberation of Italy, then, of course, one could sacrifice one's security for such a noble and sacred cause, but not for the theatre. At this point Frau Lenore grew agitated and began imploring her daughter at least not to put wrong ideas into her brother's head and be satisfied with being such a desperate republican herself! Having uttered those words, Frau Lenore began to moan and complain about her head which, she said, was 'fit to burst'. (Out of respect for their visitor, Frau Lenore spoke French to her daughter.)

Gemma began at once to humour her, fuss over her; she blew gently on her forehead, first dabbing it with eau-de-Cologne, gently kissed her cheeks, put pillows under her head, forbade her to speak—and kissed her again. Then, turning to Sanin, she began telling him in a half-jesting, half-affectionate tone of voice what a splendid mother she had and what a beautiful woman she had been! 'But what am I saying? Had been? Why, she is charming now too! Look, look, what beautiful eyes she has!'

Gemma at once pulled a white handkerchief from her pocket, covered her mother's face with it, and slowly drawing it downwards, gradually uncovered Frau Lenore's forehead, eyebrows and eyes; then she

27

paused and asked her mother to open them. Frau Lenore obeyed, Gemma uttered a cry of delight (Frau Lenore's eyes really were very beautiful), and, quickly removing the handkerchief from the lower and less regular part of her mother's face, started kissing her again. Frau Lenore laughed and, turning away a little, pushed her daughter away with a simulated effort. Gemma, too, pretended to struggle with her mother and caressed her—not like a cat, not in the French manner, but with that Italian grace in which there is always felt the presence of power.

At last Frau Lenore declared that she was tired. . . . Then Gemma at once advised her to have a little nap in her armchair, while she with the Russian gentleman, *avec le monsieur russe*, would be as quiet, as quiet—as little mice, *comme des petites souris*. Frau Lenore smiled in reply, closed her eyes and, after a few sighs, dozed off. Gemma quickly sank on to a footstool beside her and did not stir any more, only now and again putting the finger of one hand to her lips (with the other hand she was holding up the pillow behind her mother's head) and murmuring a soft 'Sh-sh!' with a sidelong glance at Sanin whenever he permitted himself the slightest movement. In the end he, too, seemed to sink into a kind of trance and sat motionless, as though bewitched, intent entirely on admiring the picture before him: the room, plunged in semi-darkness, in which, here and there, lovely, fresh roses in antique green glasses glowed brightly, the sleeping woman with demurely folded hands and a kind, tired face, framed in the snowy whiteness of the pillow, and the young, keenly alert and also kind, intelligent, pure and indescribably beautiful creature with such black, deep, shaded and yet glowing eyes. . . . What was it? A dream? A fairy-tale? And how did *he* happen to be there?

28

11

THE bell tinkled over the front door. . . . A young peasant lad in a fur cap and red jacket came into the shop from the street. Since early morning not a single customer had looked into it. . . .

'That is the sort of business we get,' Frau Lenore had said to Sanin with a sigh during lunch.

She went on dozing; Gemma was afraid to take her arm from under the pillow and whispered to Sanin: 'Go and mind the shop for me.' Sanin immediately tiptoed into the shop. The peasant lad asked for a quarter of a pound of peppermints.

'How much shall I ask?' Sanin asked Gemma in a whisper through the door.

'Six kreutzers,' she replied in the same whisper. Sanin weighed out a quarter of a pound, found some paper, made a cone out of it, put the peppermints into it, spilt them, put them in again, spilt them again, gave them to the boy at last and took the money. . . . The boy looked at him in astonishment, twirling his hat over his stomach, while in the next room Gemma, her hand pressed against her mouth, was dying of laughter. As soon as the first customer went out, another came in, then a third. . . . 'I seem to be lucky,' thought Sanin. The second customer asked for an almond drink and the third for half a pound of sweets. Sanin satisfied them, clattering the spoons with great gusto, moving saucers about and boldly putting his fingers into drawers and jars. On reckoning up, it appeared that he had charged too little for the almond drink and two kreutzers too much for the sweets. Gemma did not stop laughing surreptitiously, and Sanin too felt quite unusually gay. He was in a particularly happy mood. He felt as though he could have stood behind the counter selling sweets and soft drinks for ever while that charming creature kept looking at him through the door with affectionately mocking eyes, and the summer sun, breaking through the thick foliage of the chestnut trees growing in front of the windows, filled the whole room with the greenish gold of its noonday beams and noonday shadows, and the heart luxuriated in the sweet languor of idleness, carelessness and youth—the youth of the very young.

A fourth customer asked for a cup of coffee; Sanin had to summon Pantaleone to attend to him. (Emilio had not yet come back from Herr Klüber's shop.) Sanin sat down beside Gemma again, while Frau Lenore went on dozing, to the great delight of her daughter.

'Sleep is the best cure for my mother's migraine,' she observed.

Sanin began talking in a whisper, as before—about his 'trade' and very seriously demanded to know the prices of various confectioner's commodities; Gemma just as seriously told him what the prices were, while both of them were inwardly laughing together, as though realizing that they were acting a most amusing comedy. Suddenly an organ-grinder in the street began playing an aria from the *Freischütz*: *Durch die Felder, durch die Auen.* . . . The plaintive melody,

quivering and whistling, fell mournfully on the motionless air. Gemma gave a start. 'He'll wake Mother!'
Sanin at once rushed out into the street, thrust a few
kreutzers into the organ-grinder's hand and made him
stop playing and go somewhere else. When he returned, Gemma thanked him with a light nod of the
head and, smiling pensively, began humming softly
the beautiful melody of Weber's, in which Max ex-
presses all the perplexities of first love. Then she asked
Sanin whether he knew *Freischütz* and whether he
liked Weber, adding that though she was herself an
Italian she loved such music best of all. From Weber
their conversation turned to poetry and romanticism,
to Hoffmann, whom everybody was still reading at
that time. . . .

Frau Lenore continued to doze and even snored a
little, and the sun's rays, which broke through the
shutters in narrow shafts of light, were imperceptibly
but ceaselessly moving about and travelling across the
floor, the furniture, Gemma's dress and the leaves and
petals of the flowers.

12

I T appeared that Gemma was not too fond of Hoffmann and even found him—boring! The fantastic,
misty northern element of his stories was not easily
accessible to her bright southern nature. 'It's all fairy-
tales, it's all written for children!' she insisted, not
without contempt. She was also dimly aware of the
absence of poetry in Hoffmann. But there was one of
his stories, whose title she had forgotten, which she
liked very much; strictly speaking, it was only the beginning of this story that she liked: its ending she had
either not read or had forgotten. The story was about
a young man who somewhere—was it in a confectioner's?—meets a girl of striking beauty—a Greek
girl; she is accompanied by a mysterious, strange,
wicked old man. The young man falls in love with the
girl at first sight; she looks at him so mournfully as
though imploring him to set her free. . . . He goes out
for a moment and, on returning to the confectioner's,
finds there neither the girl nor the old man; he tries
desperately to find her, constantly comes across their
fresh tracks, chases after them, but can never by any
means find them anywhere. The beautiful girl dis-
appears from his sight for ever and ever, but, try as he
may, he cannot forget her beseeching eyes, and he is

tormented by the thought that all the happiness of his life, perhaps, has slipped through his fingers. . . .

Hoffmann could hardly have ended his story like that, but that was how Gemma believed its ending to have been, that was how it stayed in her memory.

'I believe,' she said, 'that such meetings and such partings occur in life more often than we think.'

Sanin said nothing and a little later began talking of Herr Klüber. He mentioned his name for the first time; till that moment he had not once thought of him.

Gemma said nothing in her turn and fell into thought, nibbling at the nail of her forefinger and looking away. Then she put in a good word for her fiancé, mentioned the trip into the country he had arranged for the next day, and glancing quickly at Sanin, fell silent again.

Sanin did not know after that what else to talk about.

Emilio rushed noisily into the room and wakened Frau Lenore. . . . Sanin felt relieved at his appearance.

Frau Lenore got up from her armchair. Pantaleone appeared and announced that dinner was served. The friend of the family, ex-singer and servant, also carried out the duties of a cook.

13

SANIN stayed on after dinner too. They would not let him go, still on the same excuse of the terrible heat, and when the heat abated, he was invited to go into the garden to drink coffee in the shade of the acacias. Sanin agreed. He felt very happy. There are great delights hidden in the monotonously slow and smooth current of life, and he gave himself up to them with pleasure, without demanding anything special from today, but without thinking of tomorrow, either, nor recalling the day before. What was the proximity of a girl like Gemma alone worth to him? He would soon part from her, most probably for ever; but while, as in Uhland's love song, the same skiff carried them along on the becalmed sea of life, rejoice, enjoy yourself, traveller! And everything seemed sweet and delightful to the happy traveller. Frau Lenore proposed that he should join her and Pantaleone in a game of *tresette*, and she told him how to play this uncomplicated Italian game, and won a few kreutzers from him, and he was well content; Pantaleone, at Emilio's request, made the poodle Tartaglia go through all his tricks, and Tartaglia jumped over a stick, 'spoke', that is, barked, sneezed, shut the door with his nose, fetched his master's worn-out slipper and, finally, with an old shako on

34

his head, represented Marshal Bernadotte, subjected to cruel reproaches by Napoleon for his betrayal. Pantaleone, of course, performed the part of Napoleon and he performed it very faithfully; he folded his arms across his breast, pulled a three-cornered hat over his eyes and spoke sharply and coarsely in French, but, good Lord, *what* French! Tartaglia sat before his sovereign, all contorted, with his tail between his legs, blinking embarrassedly and screwing up his eyes under the peak of his shako which was pulled sideways over his head; from time to time when Napoleon raised his voice, Bernadotte stood up on his hind legs. '*Fuori, traditore!*' cried Napoleon at last, forgetting in the excess of his exasperation that he ought to have sustained his French character to the end, and Bernadotte rushed headlong under the sofa, but at once darted out again with a joyful bark, as if to make it quite clear that the performance was at an end. All the spectators laughed a lot and Sanin most of all. Gemma had a particularly charming, continuous, quiet laugh with most amusing little shrieks. . . . Sanin was deeply moved by this laugh —he would gladly have smothered her with kisses for those little shrieks!

Night came at last. It was high time for him to go! After taking leave of everyone several times, saying again and again 'Till tomorrow' to everyone (he even kissed Emilio), Sanin went home, taking with him the image of the young girl, laughing one minute, pensive another, calm and even indifferent, but always attractive! Her eyes, sometimes wide open, bright, and sparkling as the day and sometimes half-covered by the lashes and deep and dark as night, were constantly before his eyes, strangely and sweetly pervading all other images and ideas.

Of Herr Klüber, of the reasons that made him stay in

35

Frankfort—in a word, almost of everything that had worried him the day before—he did not think even once.

14

WE must, however, say a few words about Sanin himself.

To begin with, he was most certainly a very good-looking young man. He was tall and slender, with pleasant though slightly indeterminate features and small kindly bluish eyes, golden hair, pink and white complexion and, above all, that good-humoured, gay, confiding, frank and, at the first glance, somewhat foolish expression, by which in former days one could recognize at once the children of respectable families of noblemen, 'chips of the old block', well-behaved young gentlemen, born and fattened in our wide open spaces bordering on the steppes; a somewhat faltering gait, a voice with a lisp, a smile like a child's, as soon as you looked at him and, finally, freshness, innocence, health and—softness, softness, softness—there you have the whole of Sanin. Secondly, he was not by any means stupid and he had picked up a little knowledge here and there. He had kept his freshness in spite of his trip abroad: the turbulent emotions which agitated the best part of the younger generation of those days were little known to him.

More recently, after a vain search for 'new men', young men have begun to appear in our literature who had made up their minds at all costs to be fresh, as fresh as Flensburg oysters imported into Petersburg. . . . Sanin was not like them. And if we must make use of comparisons, he reminded one most of all of a young, leafy, not long since grafted apple tree in our black-earth orchards—or better still, a well-cared-for, sleek, thick-legged, tender three-year-old in some of our former 'gentlemen's' stud farms that was only just being put through his paces by the use of the lunge. Those who happened to come across Sanin afterwards, when life had thoroughly broken him and his unnatural youthful plumpness had left him, saw in him quite a different man.

*   *   *

Next morning Sanin was still in bed when Emilio, in his Sunday best, with a cane in his hand and his hair well oiled, burst into his room and announced that Herr Klüber would soon arrive with the carriage, that the weather promised to be wonderful, that they had everything ready, but that his mother would not come with them because she had a headache again. He began to hurry Sanin, telling him that they had not a moment to lose. . . . And, to be sure, Sanin was still dressing when Herr Klüber arrived. He knocked at the door, came in, bowed, bending almost double, expressed his readiness to wait as long as might be necessary, and sat down, balancing his hat elegantly on his knees. The handsome shop manager had dressed himself up like a

37

dandy and had not spared the contents of the scent bottle: every one of his movements was accompanied by a strong whiff of the most delicate perfume. He arrived in a comfortable open carriage, a so-called landau, drawn by two tall and powerful, though far from handsome horses. A quarter of an hour later, Sanin, Klüber and Emilio drove up solemnly in this carriage to the front door of the confectioner's shop. Signora Roselli firmly refused to take part in the excursion. Gemma wanted to stay with her mother; but Signora Roselli, as they say, simply bundled her out of the house.

'I don't want anybody,' she insisted. 'I shall go to sleep. I'd send Pantaleone with you, too, but there wouldn't be anyone to mind the shop.'

'May we take Tartaglia?' asked Emilio.

'Yes, of course.'

Tartaglia at once scrambled joyfully, though not without some struggle, on to the box and sat there licking himself; one could see that he was used to it. Gemma put on a large straw hat with brown ribbons; the hat was turned down in front, shading her entire face from the sun. The line of shadow stopped just at her lips: they glowed virginally and delicately like the petals of a centifoil rose, and her teeth gleamed furtively and also innocently, as with children. Gemma sat down on the back seat beside Sanin; Klüber and Emilio sat opposite. The pale face of Frau Lenore appeared at the window. Gemma waved her handkerchief to her—and the carriage started.

15

SODEN is a little town half an hour's drive from Frankfort. It is situated in a beautiful locality in the foothills
of the Taunus mountains, and is known in Russia for its
waters, which are supposed to be beneficial to people
with weak chests. The natives of Frankfort go there
mostly for recreation, for Soden has a beautiful park
with all sorts of *Wirtschaften* where one can drink beer
and coffee in the shade of tall lime-trees and syca-
mores. The road from Frankfort to Soden runs along
the right bank of the Main and is planted on both
sides with fruit trees. While the carriage was rolling
gently along the excellent road, Sanin was stealthily
watching Gemma to see what her attitude was towards
her fiancé. It was the first time he had seen them together. *She* carried herself calmly and simply, but was
a little more reserved and serious than usual; *he* had the
air of a condescending schoolmaster who allowed himself and those under his authority a discreet and urbane
kind of pleasure. Sanin did not notice any special signs
in him of attentiveness towards Gemma, what the
French call *empressement*. It was evident that Herr
Klüber considered the matter as settled and therefore
saw no reason to be troubled or agitated. But his air of
condescension did not leave him for a single moment!

Even during their long walk before dinner along the wooded hills and dales beyond Soden, even while enjoying the beauties of nature, his attitude towards it, towards nature itself, had the same air of condescension, through which his customary magisterial severity broke every now and then. So, for instance, he remarked about one brook that it flowed too straight through the valley instead of making a few picturesque bends; nor did he approve of the conduct of a bird—a chaffinch—which had not varied her song sufficiently. Gemma was not bored; indeed, she even seemed to enjoy herself. But Sanin did not recognize the old Gemma in her; it was not as though a shadow had fallen over her—her beauty had never been more dazzling, but her soul seemed to have withdrawn into itself. Her parasol open, but without unbuttoning her gloves, she walked sedately, without hurrying, as well-brought-up young girls do—and spoke very little. Emilio, too, felt constrained, as indeed Sanin was all along. He felt, incidentally, a little put out by the fact that the conversation was always conducted in German. Tartaglia alone did not lose heart. He raced, barking furiously, after the blackbirds who happened to cross his path, leapt over ruts, tree-trunks, water-holes, flung himself into the water and lapped at it hurriedly, shook himself, yelped, and was off again like an arrow, his red tongue almost thrown over his shoulder. Herr Klüber, for his part, did everything he thought necessary for the entertainment of the whole company; he begged them to sit down in the shade of a spreading oak-tree and, producing from a side pocket a small book entitled *Knallerbsen, oder du sollst und wirst lachen!* ('Firecrackers, or you must and shall laugh!'), began reading amusing police-court anecdotes, of which the book was full. He read about a dozen of

40

them, but aroused little mirth; Sanin alone grinned out of politeness, and Klüber himself after each story emitted a brief, business-like but still condescending laugh. At twelve o'clock the whole party returned to Soden, to the best tavern in the town.

Arrangements had to be made about dinner. Herr Klüber suggested that they should have dinner '*im Gartensalon*', in the summer-house which was shut in on all sides; but at this point Gemma suddenly rebelled and declared that she would dine only in the open air, in the garden, at one of the little tables placed in front of the tavern; that she was tired of being with the same people all the time and that she wanted to see others. At some of the tables groups of newly arrived visitors were already sitting.

While Herr Klüber, giving in condescendingly to 'the caprice' of his fiancée, went to consult the head waiter, Gemma stood motionless with lowered eyes and compressed lips. She felt that Sanin was watching her persistently and, as it were, questioningly and this apparently made her angry. At last Herr Klüber came back and announced that in half an hour dinner would be ready; in the meantime he suggested a game of skittles, adding that it was very good for the appetite, heh-heh-heh! He was an excellent skittles player; as he threw the ball, he assumed quite amazingly dashing postures, smartly showing off his muscles, smartly shaking and lifting his leg. In his own way he was an athlete—and of an excellent physique! His hands, too, were so white and beautiful, and he wiped them with such a sumptuous gold-striped Indian silk handkerchief!

The moment for dinner came—and the whole company sat down at the table.

16

WHO does not know what a German dinner is like?
Watery soup with lumpy dumplings and bits of cinna-
mon, stewed beef, dry as cork with adhering white fat,
clammy potatoes, soft beetroot and grated horseradish,
a bluish eel with capers and vinegar, roast meat with
chutney, and the inevitable cooked *Mehlspeise*, a kind
of pudding with a sourish red sauce; the wine and beer,
on the other hand, are excellent. It was with just such
a dinner that the Soden innkeeper regaled his guests.
However, the dinner itself passed off satisfactorily.
There was no particular liveliness, it is true, not even
when Herr Klüber proposed the toast to 'what we
love!' (*was wir lieben!*). Everything was much too
decorous and respectable. After dinner, coffee was
served—thin, brownish, typically German coffee. Herr
Klüber, like a real gentleman, asked Gemma's permission to smoke a cigar. . . . But at this point something
happened that was quite unforeseen and decidedly unpleasant—and even indecorous! . . .

One of the nearby tables was occupied by several
officers of the Mainz garrison. From their whisperings
and glances it could be easily divined that they had
been greatly struck by Gemma's beauty; one of them,
who had probably been to Frankfort, kept looking at

her as if she were someone very familiar to him; he evidently knew who she was. He suddenly got up and, glass in hand—the officers had been drinking hard and the tablecloth in front of them was covered with bottles —went up to the table at which Gemma was sitting. He was a very young, fair-haired man, with quite a pleasant and even attractive face; but it was distorted with the wine he had drunk: his cheeks were twitching, his bloodshot eyes roved and assumed an insolent expression. His fellow-officers at first tried to restrain him, but afterwards let him go. Why not risk it? Why not see what would happen?

Slightly swaying on his feet, the army officer stopped before Gemma and announced in an unnaturally shrill voice, in which he involuntarily disclosed his own inward struggle with himself: 'I drink to the health of the most beautiful coffee-house proprietress in all Frankfort, in the whole world' (at this point he 'knocked back' his drink) 'and in return take this flower picked by her divine little fingers!' He picked up the rose which lay beside Gemma's plate. At first Gemma looked astonished, frightened, and turned terribly pale, then her fright changed into indignation, she flushed suddenly, reddening to the roots of her hair, and her eyes, looking straight at the man who had insulted her, darkened and at the same time flashing, were filled with anguish and began to burn with the fire of irrepressible anger. The officer was probably put out by her look; he muttered something inarticulate, bowed and went back to his table. His fellow-officers greeted him with laughter and light applause.

Herr Klüber suddenly rose from his chair and, drawing himself up to his full height and putting on his hat, said in a voice full of dignity, but not too loud: 'This is unheard of! Unheard-of impertinence!' (*'Unerhört!*

Unerhörte Frechheit!'), and at once summoning the waiter in a stern voice, demanded to be given his bill immediately. He did more: he ordered his carriage, adding that it was impossible for respectable people to patronize an inn where they were exposed to insults! At those words Gemma, who had remained sitting without stirring, only her bosom rising and falling violently, turned to look at Herr Klüber and—she looked at him as fixedly and with the same expression as at the officer. Emilio was simply trembling with suppressed fury.

'Get up, *mein Fräulein*,' Klüber said, with the same sternness, 'it isn't proper for you to remain here. We'll go inside and wait there!'

Gemma got up silently: he offered her his arm, she gave him hers, and he walked majestically in the direction of the inn, his gait and carriage growing more majestic and haughty the farther he got from the place where they had dined. Poor Emilio trudged miserably after them.

But while Herr Klüber was settling the bill with the waiter, whom, as a sign of his disfavour, he did not tip a single kreutzer, Sanin walked up quickly to the table at which the officers were sitting and, addressing the man who had insulted Gemma and who was just then offering her rose to his fellow-officers to smell in turn, said very clearly in French:

'What you've just done, sir, is unworthy of an honourable gentleman, unworthy of the uniform you wear—and I've come to tell you that you are an ill-mannered and impudent fellow!'

The young man jumped to his feet, but another officer, who was older, stopped him with a movement of the hand, made him sit down and, turning to Sanin, asked him also in French:

'Are you a relation, a brother, or fiancé of the girl?'

'I'm a complete stranger to her,' exclaimed Sanin. 'I'm a Russian, but I cannot stand by and see such insolence with indifference. However, here's my card and my address: your fellow-officer will find me there.'

Saying this, Sanin threw his visiting-card on the table and at the same time quickly picked up Gemma's rose, which one of the officers had dropped on his plate. The young man was about to jump up again, but his companion again checked him, saying, 'Be quiet, Dönhof!' ('*Dönhof, sei still!*') Then he got up himself and, saluting, said to Sanin, not without a touch of deference in his voice and manner, that an officer of the regiment would have the honour of calling on him at his hotel next morning. Sanin replied with a short bow, and went back quickly to his friends.

Herr Klüber pretended not to have noticed either Sanin's absence or his talk with the army officers; he was urging on the driver, who was harnessing the horses, and was very angry at his slowness. Gemma did not say anything to Sanin, either; she did not even look at him: from her knitted brows, her pale and compressed lips and her very immobility, it could be gathered that she did not feel particularly happy. Emilio alone was quite obviously anxious to talk to Sanin and find out from him what had happened. He had seen Sanin go up to the officers, he had seen him give them something white—a piece of paper, a note, a card. . . . The poor boy's heart was pounding, his cheeks blazed, he was ready to fling himself on Sanin's neck, to burst out crying or to go with him at once and make short work of all those disgusting officers! However, he controlled his impulse and contented himself with following intently every movement his noble Russian friend made.

45

The driver had at last harnessed the horses; the whole party took their places in the carriage. Emilio climbed on to the box after Tartaglia; he felt happier there and, besides, Klüber, whom he could not bear to look upon calmly, did not obtrude himself on his sight.

* * *

Herr Klüber was holding forth all the way—and holding forth alone; no one, no one objected to what he was saying, nor did anyone agree with him. He insisted in particular that they should have accepted his suggestion of dining in the privacy of the summer-house. There would have been no unpleasant incidents then! He went on to express some forceful and even liberal ideas about the unpardonable way in which the government humoured army officers, did not look after their discipline and did not show sufficient respect for the civilian element in society (*das bürgerliche Element in der Societät!*) and went on to say that in time this would give rise to discontent, from which it was only one step to revolution, a sad example of which (at this point he sighed sympathetically but sternly) was provided by France! However, he added at once that he personally had the greatest respect for the authorities and never—never!—would be a revolutionary, but he could not help expressing his—er—disapproval at the sight of such licentiousness! Then he added a few more platitudes about morality and immorality, decency and the sense of dignity! . . .

During all this diatribe, Gemma, who had not seemed to be altogether pleased with Herr Klüber even during their walk before dinner (that was why she had held herself a little aloof from Sanin and seemed to have been embarrassed by his presence), was beginning quite plainly to be ashamed of her fiancé! At the end of

46

the journey she was positively miserable and though, as before, she did not attempt to speak to Sanin, she suddenly threw an imploring glance at him. For his part, Sanin was much more sorry for her than indignant with Herr Klüber; at heart he was even half-consciously pleased with what had happened in the course of that day, even though he might well expect a challenge next morning.

This painful *partie de plaisir* came to an end at last. As he helped Gemma out of the carriage before the confectioner's shop, Sanin, without uttering a word, put the rose he had taken from the army officer into her hand. She flushed, pressed his hand and instantly hid the rose. He did not want to go in, though the evening was only just beginning. She herself did not invite him in. Besides, Pantaleone, who had come out on the front steps, declared that Frau Lenore was asleep. Emilio said goodbye shyly to Sanin; he seemed to avoid him: he admired him too much! Klüber drove Sanin to his lodgings and took leave of him stiffly. For all his self-confidence, the correctly brought-up German felt ill at ease. All of them, as a matter of fact, felt ill at ease.

In Sanin, however, this feeling, the feeling of uneasiness, soon disappeared. It was replaced by a vague, but pleasant, even rapturous mood. He paced the room, whistling, and not wishing to think of anything in particular, and very pleased with himself. . . .

17

'I'll wait for the officer till ten o'clock,' he said to himself while dressing next morning, 'and then let him come and look for me.' But Germans get up early: it had not struck nine when the waiter announced that Second Lieutenant von Richter wished to see him. Sanin quickly put on his coat and told the waiter to ask him to come in. Richter, contrary to his expectations, appeared to be a very young man, almost a boy. He tried to give an expression of gravity to his beardless face, but he could not manage it: he could not even conceal his embarrassment and, as he sat down, he tripped over his sword and nearly fell. Stammering and hesitating, he informed Sanin in bad French that he had come with a message from his friend, Baron von Dönhof; that his message was to demand from Herr von Sanin an apology for the insulting remarks he had made the day before; and that in case Herr von Sanin refused to do so, Baron von Dönhof would demand satisfaction. Sanin replied that he did not intend to apologize and was ready to give him satisfaction. Then Herr von Richter, still stammering, asked with whom, at what hour and place he would have to carry out the necessary negotiations. Sanin replied that he could come back in two hours' time and that by then he,

Sanin, would try and find a second. ('Who the hell can I get for a second?' he thought to himself meanwhile.) Herr von Richter got up and began to take his leave, but on reaching the door he stopped, as though his conscience were pricking him, and, turning to Sanin, said that his friend, Baron von Dönhof, was aware, of course, that to a certain extent—er—he was to blame for the incident of the day before and for that reason he would be satisfied with small apologies, *des exguses léchères*. To which Sanin replied that he did not intend to offer any apologies whatever, either big or small, because he did not think that he was in any way to blame.

'In that case,' said Herr von Richter, reddening even more, 'you will have to exchange friendly shots— *des goups de bisdolet à l'amiaple!*'

'That I can't understand at all,' observed Sanin. 'Are we to fire in the air or what?'

'Oh, no, of course not,' the Second Lieutenant murmured, thrown into utter confusion, 'but I thought that since it is an affair between men of honour . . . I'll have a talk with your second,' he interrupted himself and went away.

Sanin sank into a chair as soon as the German officer had gone and stared at the floor. 'What's all this about?' he thought. 'How is it that my life has suddenly taken such a turn? All my past and all my future has suddenly disappeared, gone, and all that remains is that I am going to fight someone about something in Frankfort.' He remembered a crazy aunt of his who always used to dance and sing:

> 'Little ensign,
> My dear sweetheart,
> My dearest love,
> Dance with me, my darling dove!'

And he burst out laughing and sang out as his aunt used to do: 'Little ensign, dance with me, my darling dove!'

'But,' he exclaimed in a loud voice, 'I must do something about it, I mustn't lose another moment,' and he jumped to his feet and saw Pantaleone standing before him with a note in his hand.

'I knocked several times but you did not answer and I thought you were not at home,' said the old man and handed him the note: 'It's from Signorina Gemma.'

Sanin took the note, as the saying is, mechanically, opened it and read it. Gemma wrote that she was very worried about he knew what and would like to see him at once.

'The Signorina is worried,' began Pantaleone, who evidently knew what the note was about, 'and she asked me to see what you were doing and to take you to her.'

Sanin looked at the old Italian and—pondered. A sudden idea flashed across his mind. At first it seemed strange and impossible to him.

'Yet—why not?' he asked himself.

'Monsieur Pantaleone,' he said aloud.

The old man gave a start, thrust his chin into his cravat and stared at Sanin.

'Do you know,' went on Sanin, 'what happened yesterday?'

Pantaleone chewed his lips and shook his huge quiff. 'I know.'

(Emilio had told him everything as soon as he got home.)

'Oh, you do? Well, then, an officer has just this minute left me. That impudent fellow challenges me to a duel. I've accepted his challenge. But I have no second. Would *you* like to be my second?'

Pantaleone started and raised his eyebrows so high that they disappeared under his overhanging hair.

'Have you got to fight?' he asked at last, in Italian; until then he had spoken French.

'I'm afraid so. To do otherwise would mean to disgrace myself for ever.'

'H'm—if I refuse to be your second, you'll look for another, won't you?'

'I most certainly will.'

Pantaleone looked down.

'But don't you think, Signor Zanini, that your duel would be likely to cast a slur on the reputation of a certain person?'

'I don't think so, but I'm afraid there's nothing to be done about it whatever happens.'

'H'm,' Pantaleone muttered, withdrawing completely into his cravat. 'Well, and that *verroflukto Kluberio*—what about him?' he exclaimed suddenly, tossing his head back.

'What about him? Nothing.'

'*Che!*' Pantaleone shrugged contemptuously. 'In any case,' he said at last in an unsteady voice, 'I must thank you for being able to recognize in me an honourable man—*un galant' uomo*—even in my present humble position. In so doing, you've shown yourself to be a real *galant' uomo* yourself. But I must have time to think about your proposal.'

'Time is short, my dear Cip—Cippa——'

'—tola,' the old man prompted him. 'I ask only for one hour to think it over. The daughter of my benefactors is involved in this affair, and that is why I must think it over. In an hour, in three-quarters of an hour, you will know my decision.'

'All right, I'll wait.'

51

And now—what answer am I to give Signorina Gemma?'

Sanin took a sheet of notepaper and wrote on it: 'Do not worry, my dear friend. In three hours' time I'll come to see you and everything will be explained. Thank you very much for your concern,' and gave the note to Pantaleone.

Pantaleone put it away carefully in his side pocket and once more repeating 'In an hour!' walked to the door, but he turned round suddenly, and rushing up to Sanin, seized his hand and, pressing it to his *jabot*, raised his eyes to him and exclaimed:

'Noble young man! Great heart! (*Nobil giovanotto! Gran cuore!*) Permit a weak old man (*a un vecchiotto!*) to shake your brave right hand! (*la vostra valorosa destra!*).'

Then he skipped back a little, brandished his two arms and went out.

Sanin followed him with his eyes . . . picked up a newspaper and tried to read. But in vain did his eyes run over the lines; he understood nothing.

18

An hour later the waiter again came into Sanin's room and handed him an old, soiled visiting-card with the following words on it: Pantaleone Cippatola of Varese, court singer (*cantante di camera*) to his Royal Highness the Duke of Modena. After the waiter, Pantaleone himself walked in. He had changed his clothes from top to toe. He was wearing a black frock-coat and a white piqué waistcoat, across which a pinchbeck chain was coiled fancifully; a heavy cornelian seal hung low over his narrow black breeches and he had a sash round his waist. In his right hand he carried a black hareskin hat, in his left two thick chamois-leather gloves; his cravat was tied in a broader and brighter bow than ever and in his starched *jabot* he had stuck a pin with a stone, a so-called 'cat's eye' (*œil de chat*). The forefinger of his right hand was adorned by a ring in the shape of two clasped hands with a burning heart between them. A musty smell, a smell of camphor and musk, came from the whole person of the old man; the preoccupied solemnity of his bearing would have astonished the most indifferent spectator. Sanin got up to meet him.

'I am your second,' said Pantaleone in French, bending forward with his whole body and turning his toes out like a dancer. 'I've come for instructions. Do you wish to fight to the death?'

'Why to the death, my dear Cippatola? I wouldn't take back the words I uttered yesterday for anything in the world, but I'm not a bloodthirsty villain! You'd better wait here till my opponent's second arrives. I'll go into the next room and you can make all the necessary arrangements with him. Believe me, I shall never forget the good turn you're doing me and I thank you with all my heart.'

'Honour above everything!' replied Pantaleone, sinking into an armchair without waiting for Sanin to ask him to sit down. 'If that *verroflukto spichebubbio*,' he went on, mixing German with Italian, 'if that tradesman Kluberio did not realize his plain duty and got cold feet, so much the worse for him. A contemptible fellow and that's all there is to it! As for the conditions of the duel, I'm your second and your interests are sacred to me! When I lived in Padua, a regiment of the White Dragoons was stationed there and I was on intimate terms with many of the officers! I know their entire code very well. And I've also had many talks with your Principe Tarbussky about these matters. . . . Is the other second due here soon?'

'He should be here any minute—why, here he is!' added Sanin, looking out into the street.

Pantaleone got up, looked at his watch, adjusted his quiff and hurriedly thrust into his shoe a piece of tape dangling from his breeches. The young Second Lieutenant came in, looking as red and embarrassed as ever.

Sanin introduced the seconds to each other.

'Monsieur von Richter, *souslieutenant*!'

'Monsieur Cippatola, *artiste*!'

The Second Lieutenant was a little taken aback at the sight of the old man. . . . Oh, what would he have said if anyone had whispered to him at that moment that the *artiste* he had been introduced to practised the culinary art too! But Pantaleone assumed an air as though taking part in the arrangement of a duel was the most ordinary thing to him; the memories of his theatrical career were no doubt of great assistance to him in this case; indeed, he acted the part of a second as if it were a part in a play. Both he and the Second Lieutenant were silent for a while.

'Well,' Pantaleone first broke the silence, playing with his cornelian seal, 'let's start. . . .'

'Let's start,' replied the Second Lieutenant, 'but — the presence of one of the antagonists——'

'I'll leave you at once, gentlemen,' cried Sanin and, bowing, he went into the bedroom and locked the door behind him.

He flung himself on the bed and began thinking of Gemma, but he could not help overhearing the conversation of the seconds which reached him through the locked door. They were talking in French, both mangling it unmercifully, each in his own way. Pantaleone again mentioned the dragoons in Padua and the Principe Tarbussky; and the Second Lieutenant was talking of '*exguses léchères*' and '*goups à l'amiaple*'. But the old man refused to listen to any *exguses*! To Sanin's horror, he started telling the German officer of a certain innocent young lady, whose little finger was worth more than all the officers in the world (*oune zeune damigella innoucenta, qu'a ella sola dans soun péti doa vale piu que toutt le zouffissié del mondo!*) and repeated several times heatedly: 'This is shameful! This is shameful!' ('*E ouna onta, ouna onta!*') The Second Lieutenant did not reply at first, but later an angry tremor could be heard in his voice and he observed that he had not come there to be preached at.

55

'At your age,' Pantaleone exclaimed, 'it is always useful to listen to just words!'

The argument between the seconds grew stormy several times; it went on for over an hour and at last resulted in the following agreed conditions: 'Baron von Dönhof and M. de Sanin to fight a duel with pistols the next day at ten o'clock in the morning in a small wood near Hanau at a distance of twenty paces; each of them to be entitled to two shots at a signal given by the seconds; the pistols to be single-triggered and not rifle-barrelled.' Herr von Richter then went away, and Pantaleone solemnly opened the bedroom door and, after communicating the result of the conference, exclaimed once more: '*Bravo, Russo! Bravo giovanotto!* You will be the victor!'

A few minutes later they both went to the Rosellis' shop. Sanin, however, first made Pantaleone promise to keep the affair of the duel a dead secret. In reply, the old man just raised a finger and, screwing up an eye, whispered twice over: '*Segredezza!*' He grew visibly younger and even strode along in a more carefree way. All these unusual and rather unpleasant incidents transported him vividly to the time when he himself received and gave challenges—only, it is true, on the stage. Baritones, it is a well-known fact, are very fond of strutting about in their parts.

19

EMILIO ran out to meet Sanin—he had been looking out for him for over an hour—and hurriedly whispered into his ear that his mother knew nothing of the unpleasantness of the day before, and that he should not even hint at it; that he was again being sent to Klüber's shop, but rather than go there he would hide somewhere! Having communicated this in a few seconds, he suddenly pressed himself against Sanin's shoulder, kissed it impulsively and rushed away down the street. Gemma met Sanin in the shop; she tried to say something, but couldn't. Her lips quivered and her eyes blinked and turned away. He hastened to calm her by the assurance that the whole affair had just—petered out.

'Hasn't anyone called on you today?' she asked.

'A person did call on me and we had a long talk and—and arrived at a most satisfactory arrangement.'

Gemma went back behind the counter.

'She does not believe me,' he thought, and yet he went into the next room and found Frau Lenore there.

Her migraine had passed off, but she was still in a very melancholy mood. She smiled at him amiably, but warned him at the same time that he would find her company dull that day because she was not in a fit state

57

to entertain him. He sat down beside her and noticed that her eyelids were red and swollen.

'What's the matter, Frau Lenore? You haven't been crying, have you?'

'Hush . . . ,' she whispered, motioning with her head to the room where her daughter was. 'Don't talk about it aloud!'

'But what have you been crying about?'

'Oh, Monsieur Sanin, I'm sure I don't know myself.'

'Has anyone upset you?'

'Oh no! . . . I felt very dispirited all of a sudden. I thought of Giovanni Battista . . . the days of my youth. . . . Then how quickly it has all passed away. I'm getting old, my friend, and I find it impossible to get reconciled to it. I seem to be the same as ever, and yet old age—it's here, here!' Little tears started to Frau Lenore's eyes. 'I can see you look at me and are surprised. But, my friend, you will grow old too, and you will find out how bitter it is!'

Sanin began comforting her, reminded her of her children, in whom her own youth was coming to life again, he even tried to tease her a little by assuring her that she was fishing for compliments; but she asked him quite seriously 'to stop', and he could convince himself for the first time that no words of comfort are of any avail against the despondency that comes from the consciousness of old age, and that it was impossible to dispel it; one had to wait till it had passed away of itself. He proposed a game of *tresette*—and he could not have suggested anything better. She agreed at once and seemed to cheer up.

Sanin played with her till dinner-time and after dinner Pantaleone also joined them in the game. Never had his quiff fallen so low over his forehead, never had his chin sunk so far into his cravat! His every movement exhibited such intense gravity that, looking at him, one could not help asking oneself what secret the man guarded with such firm resolution.

But *segredezza! segredezza!*

During the whole of that day he did his best to show the profoundest respect for Sanin; at table, passing over the ladies, he served him first, solemnly and resolutely; during their game he let him have additional cards and would not fine him; he declared *à propos* of nothing at all that the Russians were the most generous, brave and resolute people in the world!

'Oh, you old hypocrite!' Sanin thought to himself.

And he was not so much surprised at Signora Roselli's unexpected state of mind as at the way her daughter treated him. She did not actually avoid him; on the contrary, she always sat down not far away from him, listened to what he said, looked at him; but she most decidedly showed no inclination to get into conversation with him, and as soon as he began talking to her she would rise quietly from her seat and go out of the room for a few minutes. Then she came in again and again sat down in some corner of the room, sitting there motionless, as though sunk in thought and puzzled—puzzled most of all. Frau Lenore herself noticed at last that she was behaving in a most extraordinary way and asked her once or twice what was the matter.

'Nothing,' replied Gemma. 'You know I'm sometimes like this.'

'That's true,' her mother agreed with her.

So passed the whole of that long day, neither excitingly nor dully, neither gaily nor boringly. Had Gemma behaved differently, Sanin—who knows?—might not have been able to resist the temptation to

59

show off a little, or might simply have given way to a feeling of sadness in view of a possible parting from her, perhaps for ever. . . . But as he never succeeded in getting a word with Gemma, he had to be satisfied with striking minor chords on the piano for a quarter of an hour before evening coffee.

Emilio returned late and, to avoid being questioned about Herr Klüber, went to bed almost at once. The time came for Sanin, too, to go.

He began saying goodbye to Gemma. For some reason he recalled Lensky's parting from Olga in *Eugene Onegin*. He pressed her hand firmly and tried to look into her face, but she turned away a little and disengaged her fingers.

20

THE sky was covered with stars when he came out on the front steps. And how many stars there were in the sky—big and little, yellow, red, blue, white! . . . They all twinkled, they all swarmed, their beams sparkling as they vied with each other. There was no moon, but even without it every object could be clearly seen in the limpid shadowless twilight. Sanin walked to the end of the street. . . . He did not feel like going home at once; he felt the need to take a walk in the open air. He retraced his steps, and before he reached the house in which the Rosellis' shop was, one of the windows looking out on the street suddenly creaked and opened and in its black square (there was no light in the room) appeared a woman's figure, and he heard his name called:

'Monsieur Dimitry!'

He rushed up to the window at once—Gemma!

She was leaning against the window-sill and bent forward. 'Monsieur Dimitry,' she began in a cautious voice, 'I've wanted to give you something all day but couldn't bring myself to do so; and now, seeing you unexpectedly again, I could not help thinking that it must be fate.'

Gemma stopped involuntarily at this word. She could not go on: something extraordinary happened at that very moment.

Suddenly, amid the dead silence and in an entirely cloudless sky, there arose such a violent gust of wind that the ground seemed to tremble underfoot, the faint starlight began to quiver and shimmer, and the air itself began turning round and round in a whirlwind. The wind, not cold but warm, almost burning hot, struck the trees, the roof of the house, its walls, the street; it tore the hat from Sanin's head in an instant, and lifted and scattered Gemma's black curls. Sanin's head was on a level with the window-sill; he clung to it involuntarily and Gemma grabbed his shoulders with both hands and pressed her bosom against his head. The din, the rumble and the uproar lasted about a minute. . . . Like a flock of huge birds, the whirlwind, which arose with such suddenness, rushed away and was gone. . . . Again there was dead silence.

61

Sanin raised his head and saw above him such a lovely, frightened, excited face, such enormous, terror-stricken, magnificent eyes—he saw a girl of such great beauty that his heart stood still, he pressed his lips to a thin strand of hair that had fallen on his breast, and could only bring himself to murmur:

'Oh, Gemma!'

'What was it? Lightning?' she asked, looking round with wide-open eyes and without taking her bare arms away from his shoulders.

'Gemma!' repeated Sanin.

She sighed, cast a backward look into the room, and, with a quick movement, pulling the wilted rose out of her bodice, threw it down to Sanin.

'I wanted to give you this flower . . .'

He recognized the rose he had won back from the officers the day before.

But already the window was slammed to and he could see nothing, no white figure behind the dark window-pane.

Sanin went back home without his hat. . . . He did not even notice that he had lost it.

21

H E did not fall asleep until morning. And no wonder!
Under the impact of that sudden summer whirlwind,
he felt almost as suddenly not that Gemma was beautiful, not that he liked her—he had known that before—
but that he was almost—in love with her! Like that
whirlwind, love had swooped down on him suddenly.
And now this stupid duel! He began to be tormented
by mournful forebodings. . . . Well, suppose he were
not killed. . . . What could be the outcome of his love
for that girl, another man's fiancée? Even supposing that
he had no reason to fear 'the other man', that Gemma
herself would fall in love or had fallen in love with
him. . . . What of it? What? Such a beautiful girl. . . .

He paced the room, sat down at the table, picked up
a sheet of notepaper, traced a few lines on it and at once
crossed them out. . . . He recalled Gemma's wonderful
face in the dark window, in the starlight, her hair
blown about by the warm wind; he recalled her marble-
white arms, like the arms of the Olympian goddesses,
felt their living weight on his shoulders. . . . Then
he picked up the rose she had thrown him—and it
seemed to him that from its half-faded petals there
came another, a fragrance more subtle than the ordinary fragrance of roses. . . .

'And what if I were suddenly killed or maimed?'

He did not go to bed, but fell asleep, without undressing, on the sofa.

*　　　*　　　*

Someone tapped him on the shoulder. . . .

He opened his eyes and saw Pantaleone.

'He sleeps like Alexander of Macedon on the eve of the battle of Babylon!' exclaimed the old man.

'What's the time?' asked Sanin.

'A quarter to seven, it's a two-hour drive to Hanau and we must be the first to arrive. The Russians always forestall their enemies! I've hired the best carriage in Frankfort!'

Sanin began to wash.

'And where are the pistols?'

'The *verroflukto Tedesco* will bring the pistols. He'll bring a doctor, too.'

Pantaleone was obviously trying to pluck up courage, as he had done the day before; but when he took his seat in the carriage with Sanin, when the driver had cracked his whip and the horses started off at a gallop, a sudden change came over the old singer and friend of the Paduan dragoons. He looked embarrassed and even frightened. Something seemed to collapse in him, like a badly built wall.

'What are we doing, dear God, *santissima Madonna!*' he exclaimed in an unexpectedly squeaky voice and caught himself by the hair. 'What am I doing, old fool that I am, madman, *frenetico?*'

Sanin was surprised and laughed and, putting his arm round Pantaleone's waist, reminded him of the French proverb: *Le vin est tiré—il faut le boire.*

'Yes, yes,' replied the old man, 'we will drain this cup with you, but I'm a madman all the same. I'm a

64

madman! Everything was so quiet, so lovely, and—
suddenly: ta-ta-ta, tra-ta-ta!'

'Just like the *tutti* in an orchestra,' observed Sanin
with a forced smile. 'But it's not your fault.'

'I know it's not my fault! I should think so! But all the
same it's such—a wild, desperate act! *Diavolo! Diavolo!*'
repeated Pantaleone, shaking his quiff and sighing.

And the carriage rolled on and on. . . .

*   *   *

It was a lovely morning. The streets of Frankfort,
which had scarcely begun to stir, looked so clean and
snug; the windows of the houses flashed iridescently
like tinfoil; and as soon as the carriage had driven past
the toll-gate, the high-pitched trills of larks came pour-
ing down from above, from a blue but not yet blazing
sky. Suddenly, at a bend in the road, a familiar figure
appeared from behind a tall poplar, took a few steps and
stopped. Sanin looked more closely: Good Lord, Emilio!

'Does he know anything?' he turned to Pantaleone.

'I tell you I'm a madman,' the poor Italian cried
despairingly, almost at the top of his voice. 'The luckless boy kept worrying me all night—and this morning I told him everything at last.'

'So much for *segredezza*!' thought Sanin.

The carriage drew level with Emilio; Sanin told the
driver to pull up and called to 'the luckless boy' to
come up. Emilio, pale as on the day of his fainting fit,
came up to the carriage with hesitating steps. He could
hardly stand on his feet.

'What are you doing here?' Sanin asked him sternly.
'Why aren't you at home?'

'Let me—let me come with you, please,' Emilio
murmured in a tremulous voice, putting his hands together imploringly. His teeth were chattering as in a

F   65

fever. 'I won't be in your way—only take me, please!'

'If you have the slightest regard or respect for me,' said Sanin, 'you'll go home at once or to Klüber's shop and you won't say a word to anyone, and will wait for my return!'

'Your return,' moaned Emilio, his voice breaking on a high note, 'but if you're——'

'Emilio,' Sanin interrupted him, indicating the driver with his eyes, 'pull yourself together! Please, Emilio, go home! Do as I tell you, my friend. You say you love me. Well, I beg you!'

He held out his hand to him. Emilio bent forward, whimpered, pressed Sanin's hand to his lips and, getting off the road, ran back towards Frankfort, across the fields.

'Also a noble heart,' muttered Pantaleone, but Sanin gave him a sullen look. . . . The old man sought refuge in a corner of the carriage. He realized his guilt, and, moreover, his amazement grew with every moment: had he *really and truly* become a second, had *he* got the carriage, made all the necessary arrangements and left his peaceful abode at six o'clock in the morning? Besides, his legs were beginning to ache badly.

Sanin thought it necessary to cheer him up—and he hit the mark, he found the right word.

'Where are your former high spirits, my dear Signor Cippatola? Where's—*l'antico valor?*'

Signor Cippatola sat up and frowned.

'*L'antico valor?*' he declared in a bass voice. '*Non è ancora spento* (It is not entirely lost), *l'antico valor!!*'

He assumed a dignified air, began talking of his career, of the opera, of the great tenor Garcia—and arrived in Hanau in excellent spirits. When you think of it, there is nothing in the world stronger and—weaker than a word!

22

THE wood in which the battle was to take place was a quarter of a mile from Hanau. Sanin and Pantaleone were the first to arrive, as indeed Pantaleone had predicted; they told the driver to wait at the edge of the wood and they themselves went far into the shade of the rather thick and dense trees. They had to wait for almost an hour.

The waiting did not seem particularly wearisome to Sanin; he walked up and down the path, listened to the birds singing, watched the dragonflies as they flew past and, like the majority of Russians in similar circumstances, tried not to think. Once only did he give way to depression: he stumbled against a young lime-tree broken, in all probability, by the storm of the night before. The tree seemed to be positively dying . . . all the leaves on it were dying. 'What is it? An omen?' flashed across his mind; but he immediately began to whistle a tune, leapt over the fallen lime-tree and walked on along the path. As for Pantaleone—he grumbled, cursed the Germans, groaned, rubbed his back and then his knees. He even yawned from excitement, which lent a most comic expression to his tiny, shrunken face. Sanin nearly burst out laughing as he looked at him.

At last they heard the clatter of wheels on the soft road. 'It's them!' said Pantaleone, pricking up his ears and straightening himself, not without a momentary nervous tremor which he at once tried to conceal, however, with the exclamation, 'Brrrh!' and the remark that the air was rather chilly that morning. A heavy dew had drenched the grass and leaves, but the heat was already penetrating into the wood.

The two officers soon appeared under its canopy, accompanied by a stocky little man with a phlegmatic, almost sleepy face . . . the army doctor. He carried in one hand an earthenware jug of water just in case of need; a bag with surgical instruments and bandages dangled from his left shoulder. It was evident that he was all too familiar with such excursions; they formed one of his sources of income: each duel brought him in eight gold sovereigns—four from each of the combatants. Herr von Richter carried a case of pistols and Herr von Dönhof was twirling a little cane in his hand, which was probably just his way of showing off.

'Pantaleone,' Sanin whispered to the old man, 'if— if I'm killed—anything may happen—get the piece of paper out of my side pocket—there's a flower wrapped in it—and give it to Signorina Gemma. Do you hear? Promise?'

The old man looked gloomily at him and nodded in affirmation. . . . But goodness only knows whether he really understood what Sanin was asking him to do.

The antagonists and the seconds, as is customary, exchanged bows; the doctor alone did not turn a hair and sat down yawning on the grass, as much as to say: 'I don't give a damn about expressions of chivalrous courtesies.' Herr von Richter proposed to Mr. 'Tishibadola' to choose the site for the duel; Mr. 'Tishibadola', hardly able to move his tongue (the 'wall'

68

within him had again collapsed), replied: 'You do it, sir, I'll just watch. . . .'

And Herr von Richter set to work. Not far away in the wood he found a very beautiful clearing, all dotted with flowers, measured out the steps, marked out the two points at the opposite ends of it with hurriedly whittled sticks, took the pistols out of the case and, squatting down, rammed in the bullets; in a word, he laboured with a will, constantly mopping his perspiring face with a white handkerchief. Pantaleone, who accompanied him, looked more like a man who was chilled to the marrow. During all these preparations the two antagonists stood at some distance from one another, looking like two schoolboys who had been given a hiding and who were sulking at their masters.

The decisive moment came. . . .

'Each one his pistol took. . . .'

But at this point Richter remarked to Pantaleone that, according to the duelling rules, it was his duty as the senior second to address the two combatants with a final word of advice or a suggestion for a reconciliation before he uttered the fatal 'One, two, three!'; that although this suggestion never had the slightest effect and, as a rule, was nothing but a mere formality, yet by carrying out that formality Signor Cippatola would discharge a certain amount of his responsibility; that, as a matter of fact, such an exhortation was the direct duty of the so-called 'impartial witness' (*unpartheiische Zeuge*), but as they had no such witness, he, Herr von Richter, would readily yield that privilege to his honoured colleague. Pantaleone, who had already managed to make himself scarce behind a bush, so as not to see the army officer who had insulted his mistress, at first could not make head or tail of Herr von

Richter's speech, particularly as it had been spoken through the nose; but he suddenly gave a start, stepped forward quickly and, beating his breast convulsively, cried in a hoarse voice in his mixed jargon: '*A la la la . . . che bestialità! Deux zeun' ommes comme ça qué si battono—perché? Che diavolo? Andate a casa!*'

'I do not agree to a reconciliation,' Sanin said, hastily.

'I don't agree, either,' his opponent repeated after him.

'Well, then,' von Richter turned to Pantaleone, who was utterly at a loss what to do, 'shout: one, two, three!'

Pantaleone at once dived into the bushes again—and from there shouted, cowering, screwing up his eyes and turning away his head, at the top of his voice: '*Uno—due—tre!*'

Sanin was the first to fire—and missed. His bullet hit a tree. Baron Dönhof fired immediately after him—deliberately to one side into the air.

There was a tense silence. . . . No one stirred. Pantaleone uttered a little moan.

'Shall we go on?' said Dönhof.

'Why did you fire into the air?' asked Sanin.

'That's none of your business.'

'Will you fire into the air a second time?' Sanin asked again.

'Perhaps. I don't know.'

'Please, please, gentlemen,' began von Richter, 'duellists have no right to speak to one another. It's quite irregular.'

'I refuse to fire again,' said Sanin, throwing down his pistol.

'I do not intend to go on with the duel, either,' cried Dönhof, also throwing down his pistol. 'Moreover, I'm

70

quite willing to admit now that I was in the wrong the day before yesterday.'

He hesitated a little and then held out his hand irresolutely. Sanin approached him rapidly and shook it. The two young men looked smilingly at one another—and their faces coloured.

'*Bravi! Bravi!*' Pantaleone roared suddenly, as if he had gone mad, and clapping his hands, tumbled out of the bush; but the doctor, who had been sitting apart from the rest on a felled tree, got up at once, poured the water out of the jug and walked off swaying lazily to the edge of the wood.

'Honour is satisfied and the duel is over!' von Richter announced.

'*Fiori!*' Pantaleone shouted again from habit.

Having exchanged bows with the officers and got into the carriage, Sanin, it is true, was deeply conscious of being, if not pleased, at least greatly relieved, as after a successful operation; but another feeling, too, stirred in him, a feeling that resembled shame. . . . The duel in which he had just played his part seemed a piece of hypocrisy to him, an obviously contrived formality, the sort of thing that is all too common among army officers or students. He recalled the phlegmatic doctor, he recalled how he had smiled, that is, wrinkled up his nose, when he saw him walking out of the wood almost arm in arm with Baron Dönhof. And afterwards when Pantaleone had paid the doctor his fee of four sovereigns . . . Oh dear, there was something wrong about it all!

Yes, Sanin felt a little ashamed and conscience-stricken, though, on the other hand, what else could he have done? He could not have let the young officer's insolence go unpunished, he could not have acted like another Klüber, could he? He had taken Gemma's

71

part, he had defended her . . . that was so; and yet he felt sick at heart, he was conscience-stricken and even ashamed.

Pantaleone, on the other hand, was absolutely triumphant! He was suddenly overcome by a feeling of pride. A victorious general, returning from the field of battle he has won, could not have cast such self-satisfied glances around him. Sanin's behaviour during the duel filled him with rapture. He acclaimed him as a hero and would not listen to his admonitions and even his entreaties. He compared him to a monument of marble or of bronze—with the statue of the commander in *Don Juan*! As for himself, he admitted that he had felt a certain amount of alarm; 'but then I am an artist,' he observed. 'I am of a highly strung nature, while you are a son of the snows and the granite rocks.'

Sanin simply did not know how to damp the ardour of the artist who seemed to have lost all sense of proportion.

* * *

Almost at the same spot where two hours earlier they had come upon Emilio, he again jumped out from behind a tree and, with a joyful cry, waving his cap over his head and skipping, rushed straight at the carriage, nearly fell under the wheel and, without waiting for the horses to halt, opened the carriage door, clambered through—and gazed feverishly at Sanin.

'You're alive, you're not wounded!' he kept repeating. 'Please forgive me for disobeying you. I did not go back to Frankfort. . . . I couldn't! I waited for you here. Tell me what it was like. . . . You—you didn't kill him, did you?'

Sanin calmed Emilio with some difficulty and made him sit down.

At great length and with evident pleasure, Pantaleone retailed to him all the details of the duel, and of course did not fail to mention once again the monument of bronze and the commander's statue! He even got up and, standing with his feet wide apart to preserve his balance, folding his arms on his chest and casting scornful glances over his shoulder, he actually gave a vivid representation of the Commander Sanin! Emilio listened reverently, interrupting the story now and again with an exclamation or getting up quickly and kissing his heroic friend.

The wheels of the carriage rattled along Frankfort's cobbled streets and stopped finally before the hotel where Sanin was staying.

Accompanied by his two companions, he was mounting the stairs to the second floor when a woman suddenly walked quickly out of the dark corridor: her face was covered by a veil; she stopped dead before Sanin, swayed a little, gave a gasp and at once ran downstairs into the street and disappeared, to the great astonishment of the waiter who declared that 'that lady has been waiting for over an hour for the return of the foreign gentleman'. Momentary as her appearance was, Sanin had had time to recognize Gemma. He recognized her eyes under the thick silk of her brown veil.

'Did Fräulein Gemma know . . .' he said in a displeased voice in German, turning to Emilio and Pantaleone, who were following close upon his heels.

Emilio blushed and looked confused.

'I was forced to tell her everything,' he babbled. 'She guessed, and I just couldn't . . . But,' he went on animatedly, 'it's of no consequence now, is it? Everything has ended so wonderfully and she's seen you well and unharmed!'

Sanin turned away.

'What awful chatterboxes you are, though, the two of you!' he said with vexation and, going into his room, sat down on a chair.

'Please, don't be angry!' Emilio implored.

'Very well, I won't be angry.' (Sanin was not really angry and, after all, he could not have wished that Gemma should know *nothing*.) 'All right—stop hugging me. You can go now. I want to be alone. I'm going to sleep. I'm tired.'

'An excellent idea!' cried Pantaleone. 'You must have a rest. You have fully deserved it, noble signor! Come along, Emilio! On tiptoe! On tiptoe! Sh-sh . . .'

When he said that he wished to go to sleep, Sanin had merely wanted to get rid of his friends; but when he was left alone, he did feel tired in all his limbs. He had scarcely closed his eyes the night before. He now flung himself on his bed and fell at once into a sound sleep.

23

HE slept soundly for several hours. Then he began to dream that he was fighting another duel, that his opponent this time was Herr Klüber and that a parrot

74

was sitting on a fir-tree, and that parrot was Pantaleone, who kept tapping his beak, one-one-one! One-one-one!

'One-one-one!' he heard it a little too clearly: he opened his eyes, raised his head—someone was knocking at his door.

'Come in!' cried Sanin.

The waiter appeared and announced that a lady would very much like to see him.

'Gemma!' flashed across his mind.

But the lady was not Gemma, but her mother—Frau Lenore.

As soon as she came in, she sank into a chair and began to cry.

'What's the matter, my dear, kind Signora Roselli?' began Sanin, sitting down beside her and touching her hand with warm affection. 'What's happened? Calm yourself, I beg you.'

'Oh, Herr Dimitry, I'm very, very unhappy!'

'You're unhappy?'

'Oh, very. And how was I to expect such a thing? So suddenly, like a bolt from the blue.'

She drew breath with difficulty.

'But what is it all about? Please explain! Would you like a glass of water?'

'No, thank you.' Frau Lenore wiped her eyes with her handkerchief and began sobbing violently again. 'You see, I know everything! Everything!'

'How do you mean—everything?'

'Everything that happened today! And the reason for it—I know that too. You acted like an honourable man. But what an unfortunate combination of circumstances! I had good reason for objecting to that excursion to Soden, yes, indeed!' (Frau Lenore had said nothing of the kind on the day of the excursion, but now it seemed to her that at the time she had foreseen

75

'everything'.) 'So I've come to you, as to an honourable man, a good friend, though I only met you for the first time five days ago. . . . But, you see, I am a widow! I am all alone—my daughter——'

Tears choked Frau Lenore's voice. Sanin did not know what to think.

'Your daughter?' he repeated.

'My daughter, Gemma,' Frau Lenore burst out, almost with a moan, from behind her tear-soaked handkerchief, 'told me today that she did not want to marry Herr Klüber, and that I must refuse him!'

Sanin even started back a little: he had not expected that.

'Quite apart from the fact,' Frau Lenore went on, 'that it's a most disgraceful thing, that never before has an engagement been broken off by the girl, it means ruin to us, Herr Dimitry!' Frau Lenore carefully twisted her handkerchief tightly into a tiny little ball, as if wishing to gather up all her grief into it. 'We can't go on living any longer on the takings from our shop, Herr Dimitry! And Herr Klüber is very rich and will grow richer still. And why should I refuse him? Because he did not take his fiancée's part? I daresay it's not very nice of him, but after all, he is a civilian, he has never been to a university, and as a business man of good standing, he had to overlook the frivolous escapade of some unknown little officer. And what sort of insult was it, Herr Dimitry?'

'I'm sorry, Frau Lenore, but you seem to be blaming me. . . .'

'I'm not blaming you at all—not at all! You're quite a different matter. You are, like all Russians, a military man. . . .'

'I'm afraid I'm not at all . . .'

'You're a foreigner, a tourist, and I'm grateful to

you,' continued Frau Lenore, without listening to Sanin. She kept throwing up her hands, untwisting her handkerchief again and blowing her nose. From the way in which she expressed her grief, it could be seen that she had not been born under a northern sky.

'And how is Herr Klüber to do business in his shop if he is to fight with his customers? That's quite absurd! And now I have to refuse him. But what are we going to live on? Before, we were the only ones in Frankfort to make sweet cough mixtures and pistachio nougat, and we had lots of customers, but now everyone is making sweet cough mixtures! Just think, your duel will be talked of in the town, anyway. It couldn't be kept secret, could it? And now all of a sudden the wedding is not to take place! Why, it's a *Skandal*, a *Skandal*! Gemma is a splendid girl—she loves me very much, but she is an obstinate republican, and she snaps her fingers at what other people think of her. You alone can persuade her!'

Sanin was more astonished than ever.

'I, Frau Lenore?'

'Yes, you alone. You alone. That's why I'm here. I just couldn't think of anything else! You're so clever, so good! You have taken her part, haven't you? She trusts you! She *must* trust you, for haven't you risked your life for her? You'll make it clear, for I can't do anything more, you will make it clear to her that she is going to bring ruin on herself and all of us. You saved my son—save my daughter too! God Himself sent you here. . . . I'm ready to go down on my knees before you. . . .'

And Frau Lenore half-rose from the chair as though preparing to go down on her knees before Sanin. He restrained her.

'Frau Lenore! For God's sake, what are you doing?'

77

She grasped his hands convulsively.

'Do you promise?'

'Frau Lenore, please consider why should I——'

'You promise? You don't want me to die here now before you, do you?'

Sanin was completely at a loss what to do. It was the first time in his life that he had had to deal with a person of hot Italian blood.

'I'll do anything you like!' he cried. 'I'll talk to Fräulein Gemma . . .'

Frau Lenore uttered a joyful cry.

'Only I don't really know what the result will be . . .'

'Oh, please don't refuse me, please don't!' said Frau Lenore in an imploring voice. 'You've already given your consent! The result, I'm sure, will be excellent. Anyway, I can do no more! She won't listen to *me*!'

'Has she told you that she definitely refuses to marry Herr Klüber?' asked Sanin after a short pause.

'Yes, she nearly bit my head off! She's her father all over, like Giovann' Battista! Headstrong!'

'Headstrong? She?' Sanin repeated slowly.

'Yes—yes, but she's also an angel. She'll listen to you. Will you come soon? Oh, my dear Russian friend!' Frau Lenore got up impulsively and with the same impulsiveness threw her arms round Sanin, who was sitting opposite her. 'Accept a mother's blessing and—give me some water!'

Sanin brought Signora Roselli a glass of water, gave her his word of honour that he would come at once, escorted her down the stairs to the street and, on returning to his room, just threw up his hands and stared wildly before him.

'Well,' he thought, 'now life *has* got me whirling round in good earnest, so much so that my head's spinning round and round!' He did not even attempt to look in his heart to try to understand what was going on there: confusion, utter confusion! 'What a day!' his lips murmured involuntarily. 'Headstrong—her mother said . . . and I have to advise her—*her*? And what am I to advise her?'

Sanin's head was, in fact, in a whirl—and over all this whirl of all sorts of sensations, impressions and unfinished thoughts the image of Gemma constantly hovered—the image that had burnt itself indelibly in his memory during that warm, electrically disturbed night, in that dark window under the light of the swarming stars!

24

SANIN approached Signora Roselli's house with irresolute steps. His heart was beating violently—he felt it distinctly and could even hear it knocking against his ribs. What was he going to say to Gemma? How was he going to begin talking to her? He entered the house not through the confectioner's shop, but by the back door. In the small ante-room he came across Frau Lenore. She was glad to see him, but at the same time she was frightened too.

'I was waiting, waiting for you,' she said in a whisper, squeezing his hand with each of her hands in turn. 'Go into the garden; she is there. I rely on you, mind!'

Sanin went into the garden.

Gemma was sitting on a garden seat near the path, picking out the ripest cherries from a basket and putting them on a plate. The sun was low—it was seven o'clock in the evening—and there was more purple than gold in the wide slanting rays with which it flooded Signora Roselli's little garden. Every now and then the leaves, as though in no hurry, whispered among themselves in hushed voices, and the late bees kept up an intermittent buzzing as they flew from flower to flower, and somewhere a turtle-dove cooed and cooed—monotonously and unceasingly.

Gemma wore the same round hat in which she had driven to Soden. She glanced at Sanin from under its turned-down brim and bent over the basket again.

Sanin went up to Gemma, involuntarily slowing down every step and—and—and found nothing better to say than to ask her why she was picking out the cherries.

Gemma was in no hurry to reply.

'These are riper,' she said at last, 'and we shall be making jam with them, and the others are for pies. You know the round cherry pies we sell, with sugar on top, don't you?'

Having said this, Gemma bent her head even lower and her right hand, with two cherries between her fingers, stopped in mid-air between the basket and the plate.

'May I sit down beside you?' asked Sanin.

'You may.'

Gemma moved a little to make room for him on the seat. Sanin sat down beside her. 'How am I to begin?'

80

he wondered. But Gemma helped him out of his difficulty.

'You fought a duel today,' she said with animation and turned her beautiful face to him, shyly blushing — and how gratefully her eyes shone! 'And you're so calm! Does it mean that you're not afraid of danger?'

'Good heavens, I have not been exposed to any danger. It all turned out most satisfactorily and innocuously.'

Gemma moved a finger to the right and left in front of her eyes. Also an Italian gesture.

'No, no! Don't say that! You won't deceive me! Pantaleone has told me everything!'

'Just the man to believe! Did he compare me to the statue of the commander?'

'His expressions may be funny, but his feelings are not funny, nor what you have done today. And all because of me — for me. I shall never forget it.'

'I assure you, Fräulein Gemma . . .'

'I shall not forget it,' she repeated slowly, glancing intently at him again, and turned away.

He could now see her delicate, pure profile and it seemed to him that he had never seen anything like it and — had never experienced anything like what he was feeling at that moment. His soul was ablaze.

'And what about my promise?' it flashed across his mind.

'Fräulein Gemma,' he began after a moment's hesitation.

'What?'

She did not turn to him, she continued to sort the cherries, carefully picking up their stalks with the tips of her fingers and solicitously picking out the leaves. . . . But how intimate and caressing was the tone in which she uttered that word: 'What?'

'Hasn't your mother said anything to you about—'
'About?'
'About me?'

Gemma suddenly threw the cherries she had picked up back into the basket.

'Has she been talking to you?'
'Yes.'

'What has she been saying to you?'

'She told me that you—that you've suddenly decided to—to change your—former intentions.'

Gemma again lowered her head. She disappeared completely underneath her hat; only her neck, slender and supple as the stalk of a big flower, could be seen.

'What intentions?'

'Your intentions—concerning the future arrangement of your life.'

'You mean . . . Are you referring to—Herr Klüber?'
'Yes.'

'Did Mother tell you that I did not want to be Herr Klüber's wife?'
'Yes.'

Gemma moved forward on the seat. The basket tipped over and a few cherries rolled down on to the path. One minute passed . . . another . . .

'Why did she tell you that?' he heard her voice asking.

Sanin, as before, could see only Gemma's neck. Her bosom rose and fell more rapidly than before.

'Why? Your mother thought that as we've become friends, if I may say so, in such a short time, and as you've shown that you trusted me—er—to a certain extent, I mean, I should be able to give you some good advice and—that you would listen to me.'

Gemma let her hands fall and lie quietly on her lap. . . . She began fingering the folds of her dress.

82

'What advice are you going to give me, Monsieur Dimitry?' she asked after a short pause.

Sanin saw that Gemma's fingers were trembling in her lap. . . . She was only fingering the folds of her dress to conceal their trembling. He gently laid his hand on those pale, trembling fingers.

'Gemma,' he said, 'why don't you look at me?'

She instantly threw her hat back over her shoulders and fixed her eyes on him, trusting and grateful as before. She waited for him to speak. . . . But the sight of her face confused and almost blinded him. The warm glow of the evening sun illumined her youthful head—and the expression of that head was brighter and more luminous than its glow.

'I will listen to you, Monsieur Dimitry,' she began, smiling faintly and faintly lifting her brows, 'but what advice are you going to give me?'

'What advice?' repeated Sanin. 'You see, your mother is of the opinion that to break off your engagement to Herr Klüber only because he did not show any particular courage the other day. . .'

'Only because of that?' said Gemma and, bending down, she picked up the basket and put it on the seat beside her.

'That—in general—to break off your engagement to him is unwise on your part; that it is a step all the consequences of which must be carefully weighed— that, finally, the very position of your affairs imposes certain obligations on every member of your family.'

'All that is Mother's opinion,' Gemma interrupted. 'Those are her words. I know that. But what is your opinion?'

'Mine?' Sanin was silent for a minute. He felt a lump rising in his throat and choking him. 'I, too, think,' he began with an effort.

Gemma sat up.

'Too? You—too?'

'Yes. . . . I mean . . .' Sanin could not, positively could not add another word.

'Very well,' said Gemma, 'if, as a friend, you advise me to change my decision . . . that is, not to change my previous decision, I will think it over.' Without being aware of it, she began putting the cherries back from the plate into the basket. 'Mother hopes that I will listen to you. . . . Well, perhaps I really will. . . .'

'But, please, Fräulein Gemma, I'd first like to know the reasons which made you . . .'

'I will listen to you,' repeated Gemma, while her cheeks grew paler and paler, her brows became more and more contracted, and she began to bite her lower lip. 'You've done so much for me that I'm bound to do what you wish: bound to carry out your wishes. I'll tell Mother I'll think it over. . . . Here she is, by the way — she's coming here.'

And, indeed, Frau Lenore appeared at the door leading from the house to the garden. She was devoured with impatience: she could not keep still for a moment. According to her calculations, Sanin ought to have finished his talk with Gemma long ago, though actually his conversation with her had not lasted a quarter of an hour.

'No, no, no, for God's sake don't say anything to her yet,' Sanin said in haste, almost in alarm. 'Wait, I'll tell you, I'll write to you . . . and till then don't make up your mind about anything—wait!'

He squeezed Gemma's hand, jumped up from the seat and, to Frau Lenore's great astonishment, darted past her, raising his hat and muttering something indistinctly, and disappeared.

She went up to her daughter.

'Tell me, please, Gemma . . .'

Gemma suddenly got up and embraced her mother. 'Dear Mother, can you wait a little, just a little bit . . . till tomorrow? You can? And not a word till tomorrow? Oh, dear!'

She burst suddenly into happy tears. It was something she herself did not expect. This surprised Frau Lenore, the more so as the expression on Gemma's face was far from sorrowful, but rather joyful.

'What's the matter with you?' she asked. 'I've never seen you crying before—and now all of a sudden——'

'It's nothing, Mother, nothing. You just wait! We must both wait. Don't ask me anything till tomorrow —and let's sort out the cherries before the sun has set.'

'But will you be sensible?'

'Oh, I'm very sensible!'

Gemma shook her head significantly. She began tying up small bunches of cherries, holding them high over her blushing face. She did not wipe away her tears: they had dried of themselves.

25

SANIN returned to his hotel almost at a run. He felt, he realized, that only there, only alone with himself, would he be able to find out at last what was the matter with him, what was happening to him. And, to be sure, as soon as he entered his room, as soon as he sat down at the writing-desk, he cried, leaning his elbows on the desk and pressing his hands to his face, in a sad and hollow voice: 'I love her, I love her madly!' and he glowed inwardly, like a piece of burning coal from which the thick layer of dead ashes had been suddenly blown off. Another moment—and he was quite unable to understand how he could have sat beside her—*her!* —and talked to her and not felt that he adored the very hem of her dress, that he was ready, as young men express it, 'to die at her feet'. His last meeting with her in the garden had decided everything. Now when he thought of her, he did not see her with wind-tossed curls, in the radiance of the stars, he saw her sitting on the garden seat, saw her flinging back her hat and look-ing at him so trustingly . . . and a tremor, and the crav-ing for love ran through all his veins. He remembered the rose, which he had been carrying about in his pocket for three days: he pulled it out—and pressed it to his lips with such feverish force that he could not help contracting his brows with pain. Now he no longer reasoned, argued, calculated or foresaw anything; he had become entirely detached from all his past, he leapt forward: from the dreary shore of his lonely bachelor life he plunged headlong into that joyous, boiling, mighty torrent—and he did not care any more, he did not want to know where it would carry him or whether it would dash him to pieces against a rock! Those were no longer the gentle streams of an Uhland love song which had lulled him to sleep not long ago. . . . Those were mighty, irresistible torrents! They fly and leap forward—and he flies along with them!

He took a sheet of paper and without blotting a word, almost with one sweep of the pen, wrote as follows:

'Dear Gemma,
   You know what advice I undertook to give you, you know what your mother desires and what she asked me to do, but what you do not know and what I am in duty bound to tell you now is that—I love you, that I love you with all the passion of a heart that loves for the first time! This fire blazed up in me suddenly, but with such force that I can't find words in which to describe it!! When your mother came to see me and put her request to me, it was only smouldering in me, or else, as an honourable man, I should most certainly have refused to carry out her errand. . . . The confession I am making to you now is the confession of an honourable man. You must know with whom you are dealing—there must be no misunderstandings between us. You see that I can't give you any advice. . . . I love you, love you, love you—

and I have nothing else—either in my mind or in my heart!

D. P. Sanin'

Having folded and sealed his note, Sanin was about to ring for the waiter and send him with it. 'No, that's awkward. By Emilio? But to go to the shop and look for him among the other shop assistants would also be awkward. Besides, it is already dark and he has probably left the shop.' While trying to make up his mind what to do, Sanin put on his hat and went out into the street. After turning one corner then another, he suddenly, to his indescribable delight, saw Emilio in front of him. The young enthusiast was hurrying home, with a bag under his arm and a roll of papers in his hand.

'People say with good reason that every lover has a lucky star,' thought Sanin, and called to Emilio.

Emilio turned round and immediately rushed up to him.

Sanin gave him no time to express his delight at seeing his hero, handed him the note and explained to whom and how to deliver it. Emilio listened attentively.

'So that no one should see?' he asked, assuming a significant and mysterious air: 'We understand what it is all about!' it implied.

'Yes, my friend,' said Sanin, looking a little put out, but patting Emilio on the cheek. 'And if there is an answer, you'll bring it to me, won't you? I shall be at home.'

'Oh, don't worry about that!' Emilio whispered gaily and as he rushed off he winked at him again.

Sanin returned home and, without lighting a candle, flung himself down on the sofa, put his hands behind his head and abandoned himself to those sensations of newly awakened love which it would be a waste of time to describe: he who has experienced them knows how sweet and languorous they are; to him who has not experienced them they are impossible to explain.

The door opened and Emilio's head appeared.

'Brought it,' he said in a whisper. 'Here it is, the answer.'

He showed and held above his head a folded piece of paper.

Sanin jumped up from the sofa and snatched it out of Emilio's hands: his passion was too strong—he did not try to conceal it or to keep up appearances—even before this boy, before her brother; he would have been ashamed to show his feelings before him, he would have forced himself not to—if he could!

He went up to the window and by the light of the street lamp, which stood in front of the house, he read the following lines:

'I beg you, I implore you, *do not come to see us and do not show yourself all day tomorrow*. It's necessary, very necessary for me—and after that everything will be decided. I know you will not refuse me because . . .

Gemma'

Sanin read the note twice—oh, how touchingly sweet and beautiful did her handwriting seem to him! He thought it over a little, and turning to Emilio who, wishing to show what a discreet young man he was, was standing with his face turned to the wall, scratching it with a fingernail, called him aloud by name.

Emilio at once ran up to Sanin.

'What would you like me to do?'

'Listen, my friend——'

'Monsieur Dimitry,' Emilio interrupted him in a

plaintive voice, 'why don't you call me by my Christian name?'

Sanin laughed.

'All right. Now listen, Emilio' (Emilio jumped with pleasure), 'listen, *there*, you understand, *there* you will say that everything will be done exactly as requested' (Emilio compressed his lips and nodded importantly), 'and as for me—what are you doing tomorrow?'

'Me? What am I doing? What do you want me to do?'

'If you can, I'd like you to come here early in the morning and we'll go for a walk in the country round Frankfort. . . . Would you like that?'

Emilio gave another little jump.

'Oh, I say, what could be better? Go for a walk in the country with you—why, it's simply wonderful! I'll certainly come!'

'But what if they won't let you?'

'They will!'

'Listen, Emilio, don't tell them *there* that I asked you to spend the whole day with me.'

'Why should I? I'll get away without telling them. It won't matter a bit!'

Emilio kissed Sanin affectionately and ran off.

Sanin kept pacing the room for a long time and went to bed late. He gave himself up to the same thrilling, sweet sensations, to the same breathlessly joyful anticipation of a new life. Sanin was very glad to have hit on the idea of inviting Emilio to spend the day with him; he bore a striking resemblance to Gemma. 'He'll remind me of her,' he thought.

But what astonished him most of all was how he could possibly have been different yesterday from what he was now. It seemed to him that he had *always* loved Gemma, and that he had loved her as much as he loved her that day.

26

NEXT day, at eight o'clock in the morning, Emilio
appeared at Sanin's hotel, with Tartaglia on a lead. If
he had had German parents, he could not have been
more punctual. At home he had told a lie: he had said
he was going for a walk with Sanin until lunch-time,
and then coming back to the shop. While Sanin was
dressing, Emilio tried to talk to him, a little hesitantly,
it is true, about Gemma and her quarrel with Herr
Klüber; but Sanin kept sternly silent in reply and
Emilio, looking as though he understood why one must
not touch lightly on such an important subject, did not
return to it, and only occasionally assumed a rapt and
even severe expression.

After having coffee, the two friends set off, on foot
of course, to Hausen, a small village not far from
Frankfort, which was surrounded by woods. The entire range of the Taunus mountains could be clearly
seen from there. The weather was beautiful; the sun
was shining brightly. It was warm and not too hot; a
cool breeze rustled briskly among the green leaves; the
shadows of the high, round clouds skimmed smoothly
and swiftly in small patches over the earth. The young
men soon left the town and walked jauntily and gaily
along the well-kept road. They went into the woods

and spent a long time wandering about there; then they had a good lunch in a village inn; then climbed some mountains, admired the views, rolled stones down the mountain-side and clapped their hands as they watched the amusing and strange way in which the stones hopped about like rabbits, until a man, walking below and invisible to them, swore at them in a loud and ringing voice; they then lay spreadeagled on the short, dry moss of yellowish-violet tint; then they drank beer at another inn, then they ran races and tried for a wager to see who could jump the farthest. They discovered an echo and held a conversation with it; they sang songs, hallooed, wrestled, broke off twigs, decorated their hats with fern and—even danced. Tartaglia took part in all these pastimes as far as he could: he did not, it is true, throw stones, but he did somersault after them; he howled when the young men were singing, and even drank beer, though with undisguised aversion: a student, to whom he had once belonged, had taught him that art. He did not obey Emilio very promptly, as he did his master Pantaleone, and when Emilio ordered him 'to speak' or 'to sneeze', he only wagged his tail and hung out his tongue.

The young men also conversed with one another. At the beginning of their walk, Sanin, as the elder and therefore more thoughtful of the two, started talking about the meaning of fate or predestination and the significance and purport of man's vocation; but their conversation soon took a less serious turn. Emilio began asking his friend and patron about Russia, about how duels were fought there, whether the women there were beautiful, how long it took to learn Russian, and what he felt when the officer took aim at him. Sanin, in his turn, asked Emilio about his father and mother, and about their family affairs in general, trying his utmost not to mention Gemma's name, and thinking only of her. Actually, he was not thinking of her, but of the next day, of that mysterious tomorrow, which would bring him unknown and ineffable happiness! It was as though a curtain, a light, thin curtain, hung faintly swaying before his inner eye; and behind that curtain he felt—he felt the presence of a young, motionless, divine face with a tender smile on her lips and stern, feignedly stern, lowered eyelids. And this face was not the face of Gemma but the face of happiness itself! For now at last *his* hour had come, the curtain had risen, the lips were parting, the eyelashes were raised—the divine being had seen him—and there was at once light as from the sun, and joy, and bliss everlasting! He thought of that tomorrow—and again his heart stood still joyfully in the melting yearning of ever-renewed expectation!

And this yearning, this expectation did not interfere with anything he did. It accompanied his every movement, and did not interfere with anything. It did not prevent him from having an excellent dinner with Emilio at a third inn, and only occasionally, like a brief flash of lightning, did the thought cross his mind—What if anyone in the world knew? This yearning did not prevent him from having a game of leap-frog with Emilio after dinner. They played it on an open green meadow . . . and how great was Sanin's consternation and confusion when, to the accompaniment of Tartaglia's furious barking, his legs expertly spread out and flying like a bird over Emilio, who was bent double, he suddenly saw before him, at the farthest end of the green meadow, two army officers, in whom he recognized at once his adversary of the day before and his second, von Dönhof and von Richter! Each of them had screwed a monocle in his eye and was looking at him and grinning. . . . Sanin fell on his feet, turned away, quickly put on the overcoat he had thrown down, ejaculated a word to Emilio, who also put on his tunic, and both at once walked away.

It was late when they returned to Frankfort.

'They're sure to scold me,' Emilio said to Sanin as he said goodbye to him, 'but I don't care! I've had such a wonderful day!'

When he got back to his hotel Sanin found a note from Gemma. She fixed a meeting with him at seven o'clock on the following morning in one of the public parks which surround Frankfort on all sides.

How his heart quailed! How glad he was to have obeyed her implicitly! And, dear Lord, what—what did that day hold in store for him—that unparalleled, impossible, unique day, the tomorrow that was quite certain to come!

He gazed and gazed at Gemma's note. The long, elegant flourish of the letter 'G', the first letter of her name, at the bottom of the sheet of notepaper, reminded him of her beautiful fingers, her hand. . . . The thought occurred to him that he had never touched that hand with his lips. . . . 'Italian girls,' he thought, 'contrary to what one hears about them, are modest and severe. . . . And Gemma most of all! A queen . . . a goddess—pure, virginal marble. . . .

'But the time will come—and it isn't far off. . . .'

There was that night one happy man in Frankfort; he was asleep, but he could have said of himself in the words of the poet: 'I sleep . . . yet my sentient heart sleeps not. . . .'

Its beating was as light as the beating of the wings of a butterfly as it clings to a flower and is drenched in summer sunshine.

27

SANIN woke up at five o'clock, at six he was dressed, and at half-past six he was walking about in the public park within sight of the small summer-house Gemma had mentioned in her note.

It was a calm, warm, overcast morning. It sometimes seemed as if it would start raining any moment; but the outstretched hand felt nothing and only by looking at one's sleeves did one notice traces of drops as tiny as the minutest beads; but those, too, soon ceased. Wind—it was as though there had never been a breath of it in the world. Sounds did not come flying at you, but spread gently all around; in the distance a whitish mist was slowly condensing, the air was full of the scent of mignonette and white acacia blossoms.

In the streets the shops were not yet open, but there were already pedestrians about. From time to time there was the clatter of a solitary carriage—there were no strollers in the park. A gardener was leisurely scraping the path with a spade, and a decrepit old woman in a black woollen cloak limped across an avenue. Not for a single moment could Sanin mistake that poor old creature for Gemma—and yet his heart missed a beat and he followed the disappearing black spot attentively with his eyes.

Seven—the clock on the tower chimed hollowly.

Sanin stopped dead. Wouldn't she come after all? A cold tremor suddenly ran through his limbs. The same kind of tremor again passed over his body, but this time for a different reason. Sanin heard light footsteps behind him and the faint rustle of a woman's dress. . . . He turned round—it was she!

Gemma was walking behind him along the path. She wore a greyish cloak and a small dark hat. She glanced at Sanin, turned her head away and, as she came alongside him, walked rapidly past him.

'Gemma,' he said, in a scarcely audible voice.

She gave him a light nod and continued to walk along in front. He followed her.

He breathed in broken gasps. His legs almost refused to obey him.

Gemma walked past the summer-house, turned to the right, went past a small, shallow pool in which a sparrow was busily splashing himself and, walking behind a clump of high lilacs, sat down on a bench. It was a cosy and shut-in spot. Sanin sat down beside her.

A minute passed, and neither he nor she uttered a word; she did not even look at him, while he looked not at her face but at her folded hands in which she held a small parasol. What was there to say? What could they have said which could compare in importance with the fact that they were there, together, alone, so early, so close to each other?

'You—you are not angry with me?' Sanin said at last.

Sanin could not have said anything more foolish than these words—he realized it himself. But at least the silence had been broken.

'Me?' she replied. 'Whatever for? No.'

'And you believe me?' he went on.

96

'You mean what you wrote in your note?'

'Yes.'

Gemma lowered her head and said nothing. The parasol slipped out of her hands. She caught it hastily before it dropped on the path.

'Oh, believe me, believe what I wrote to you,' exclaimed Sanin; all his timidity suddenly disappeared — he spoke with heat: 'If there is truth on earth, sacred, undeniable truth, it is that I love you, that I love you passionately, Gemma!'

She cast an oblique, quick glance at him, and once again nearly dropped her parasol.

'Believe me, believe me,' he kept repeating. He implored her, stretched out his hands to her, and dared not touch her. 'What do you want me to do to — convince you?'

She glanced at him again.

'Tell me, Monsieur Dimitry,' she began, 'the day before yesterday when you came to persuade me, you did not, I suppose, know then — you didn't feel——'

'I did feel,' Sanin declared, 'but I did not know. I fell in love with you from the first moment I saw you, but I did not realize at once what you meant to me! Besides, I heard that you were engaged to be married. ... As for your mother's commission, in the first place I couldn't refuse it, could I? And, secondly, I believe I told you about it in such a way that you could have guessed ...'

There was the sound of heavy footsteps and a rather stout gentleman with a travelling-bag over his shoulder, quite obviously a foreigner, appeared from behind the clump of lilacs and, with the unceremoniousness of a tourist, threw a glance at the couple on the seat, cleared his throat loudly and — walked on.

'Your mother,' said Sanin, as soon as the sound of the

H 97

heavy footsteps had died away, 'told me that your refusal would cause a scandal' (Gemma frowned slightly), 'that I myself was partly responsible for the unseemly gossip and that—consequently—it was to some extent my duty to persuade you not to break off your engagement to your fiancé, Herr Klüber. . . .'

'Monsieur Dimitry,' said Gemma, passing her hand over her hair on the side turned towards Sanin, 'please, don't call Herr Klüber my fiancé. I shall never be his wife. I have broken off my engagement to him.'

'You have? When?'

'Yesterday.'

'Did you tell him?'

'Yes, I did. At home. He came to see us.'

'Gemma, so you do love me!'

She turned to him.

'Would I have come—otherwise?' she whispered, and her hands dropped on to the seat.

Sanin seized those helpless hands, lying with the palms upwards, and pressed them to his eyes, to his lips. . . . That was when the curtain he had dreamt of the night before went up. Here was happiness, here was its radiant, divine image!

He raised his head and looked at Gemma, frankly and boldly. She also looked at him—a little downwards. There was a faint gleam in her half-closed eyes, filled with light, happy tears. But her face was not smiling—no! It laughed, also with happy, though silent, laughter.

He wanted to press her to his breast, but she would not let him and, without ceasing to laugh the same silent laughter, shook her head. 'Wait!' her happy eyes seemed to say.

'Oh, Gemma,' cried Sanin, 'I never imagined, my darling' (his heart trembled like a violin string when his lips pronounced this 'darling' for the first time) 'that you would fall in love with me!'

'I did not expect it myself,' Gemma said softly.

'How could I have imagined,' Sanin went on, 'when driving into Frankfort where I planned to stay only a few hours, that I would find here the happiness of all my life?'

'All your life? Are you sure?' asked Gemma.

'All my life,' Sanin exclaimed with fresh passion, 'for ever and ever. . . .'

The gardener's spade could suddenly be heard scraping away within two paces from the bench on which they were sitting.

'Let's go home,' whispered Gemma. 'Let's go together—do you want to?'

If she had said at that moment: 'Throw yourself in the sea—*do you want to?*' he would have thrown himself headlong into the ocean before she had uttered the last word.

They went out of the park together and walked in the direction of Gemma's house, not along the city streets, but through the suburbs.

28

SANIN sometimes walked beside Gemma and sometimes a little behind her, without taking his eyes off her
and without ceasing to smile. She seemed to be in a
hurry, and yet she would stop from time to time. To
tell the truth, both of them—he very pale and she all
rosy with excitement—walked along as though in a
dream. What they had done—the two of them—a few
moments before—that surrender of one soul to another
soul—was so intense, and new, and frightening; everything in their lives had undergone so complete and so
sudden a change that they could not recover themselves, and all they were conscious of was that they had
been caught up by a whirlwind, like the whirlwind that
had nearly flung them into each other's arms that
night. Sanin walked along feeling that he was even
looking at Gemma in a different way: he instantly
noticed several peculiarities in the way she walked, in
her movements—and, dear Lord!—how infinitely
sweet and dear they were to him! And she felt that he
was looking at her *like that*.

Sanin and she had fallen in love for the first time—
and they were experiencing all the miracles of first
love. First love is like a revolution: the monotonously
regular routine of life is smashed and destroyed in one

instant, youth takes up its stand on the barricade, its bright banner flutters high—and whatever awaits it in the future—death or a new life—it sends its ecstatic greeting to everything.

'Hullo! It isn't our old man, is it?' said Sanin, pointing to a muffled figure which was hurrying along stealthily as though trying to remain unobserved. In his present state of overwhelming happiness he felt a need to speak to Gemma not of love—that was a matter that had been settled once and for all, that was sacred —but of something else.

'Yes, it's Pantaleone,' Gemma replied gaily and happily. 'I expect he must have followed me out of the house. He was watching me like a hawk all day yesterday. . . . I suppose he knows. . . .'

'He knows!' Sanin repeated delightedly.

What could Gemma have said that would not have delighted him?

Then he asked her to tell him everything that had taken place the day before.

And she began telling him at once, rapidly, confusedly, smiling, breathing fast and exchanging quick, bright glances with Sanin. She told him how after their talk the day before yesterday her mother had kept trying to find out something positive from her, Gemma; how she had put off Frau Lenore with the promise to let her have her decision within twenty-four hours; how she had obtained that delay—and how difficult it had been; how quite unexpectedly Herr Klüber had appeared, looking more starched and strait-laced than ever; how he had expressed his indignation at the childish, unpardonable and, so far as he, Klüber, was concerned, deeply insulting (that was exactly how he expressed it) escapade of the Russian stranger—'he was referring to your duel, darling'—and how he demanded that *you* should be forbidden the house at once. 'Because,' he had added—and here Gemma slightly mimicked his voice and manner—'it casts a slur on my honour. As if I couldn't have defended my fiancée if I had thought it necessary or advisable! All Frankfort will know tomorrow that a stranger has fought a duel with an officer for my fiancée—why, it's unheard of! It reflects on my honour!' Mother agreed with him—can you imagine it? But at this point I spoke up and told him straight that he need not worry about his honour or about his person and that he need not feel insulted about the gossip about his *fiancée*—because I was no longer his fiancée, and I would never be his wife! I confess I should have liked to talk it over with you first—with you, darling—before breaking off my engagement finally. But he came, and I could not restrain myself. Mother was so shocked that she screamed at me, but I went into the next room, got his ring—you didn't notice I took it off two days ago, did you?—and gave it back to him. He was terribly hurt, but as he is terribly conceited and self-satisfied, he did not make a fuss about it and—went away. Of course, I had to put up with a lot from Mother, and I was very sorry to see how much she had taken it all to heart. I couldn't help wondering if I hadn't been a little too hasty. But I had your note, you see, and, besides, I knew anyway . . .'

'That I love you?' Sanin put in.

'Yes, that you'd fallen in love with me.'

So spoke Gemma, faltering and smiling, and lowering her voice or falling silent altogether every time someone came walking towards her or passed by. Sanin listened rapturously, delighting in the sound of her voice as the day before he had been admiring her handwriting.

'Mother is terribly upset,' Gemma began again, and

her words followed very fast one upon the other. 'She refuses to take into consideration the fact that I could get sick and tired of Herr Klüber, that I was not marrying him for love, but because she had kept begging me to marry him again and again. . . . She suspects you—you, darling; I mean, she is sure I'm in love with you, and she resents it all the more because only the day before yesterday nothing of the kind had occurred to her and she even asked you to persuade me to do as she wished. . . . It was a strange request, wasn't it? Now she calls you, darling, a sly, cunning man. She says that you betrayed her confidence and she predicts that you will deceive me. . . .'

'But, Gemma,' cried Sanin, 'didn't you tell her that——'

'I told her nothing! What right had I, without talking things over with you?'

Sanin threw up his hands in astonishment.

'Gemma,' he said, 'I hope that now at least you will tell her everything and take me to her. . . . I want to prove to your mother that I'm not a deceiver!'

Sanin's chest fairly heaved from an upsurge of generous and ardent feelings.

Gemma looked at him in surprise.

'Do you really want to go with me to my mother now? To my mother who is quite sure that—that all this is quite impossible between us and that—that you will never—'

There was one word which Gemma had not the courage to utter. . . . It seared her lips; but Sanin uttered it all the more eagerly.

'Marry you, Gemma, be your husband—I don't know of any greater happiness!'

At this moment he knew of no limits to his love, his generosity, his determination.

103

When she heard him say that Gemma, who had stopped dead for a moment, quickened her pace. . . . She seemed anxious to run away from this too great and unexpected happiness!

But suddenly her legs gave way under her. Round the corner of a side-street, a few paces from her, Herr Klüber hove in sight wearing a new hat and a new long, pleated overcoat, straight as an arrow, and curled as a poodle. He saw Gemma, he saw Sanin and, with a kind of inward snort and bending back his supple waist, he strode dashingly towards them. Sanin winced, but glancing at Klüber's face, to which its owner tried, as much as he could, to give an expression of contemptuous astonishment and even commiseration—glancing at that ruddy, vulgar face, he felt an upsurge of sudden anger and took a step forward.

Gemma seized his arm, and, putting hers through it with calm determination, she looked her former fiancé full in the face. . . . Klüber screwed up his eyes, flinched, darted out of their way and, muttering through his teeth: 'The usual end to the song!' ('*Das alte Ende vom Liede!*')—walked away with the same dashing, slightly skipping walk.

'What did he say, the scoundrel?' asked Sanin, who was about to rush after Klüber.

But Gemma restrained him and walked on with him, without taking away the arm she had put through his.

Roselli's shop was now in front of them. Gemma stopped again.

'Dimitry, Monsieur Dimitry,' she said, 'we haven't gone in yet. We haven't seen Mother yet. . . . If you want to think it over a little longer, if—you're still free, Dimitry!'

In reply Sanin pressed her hand very tightly to his breast—and drew her forward after him.

'Mother,' said Gemma, as she and Sanin entered the room in which Frau Lenore was sitting, 'I've brought the real one!'

29

IF Gemma had said that she had brought cholera or death itself with her, Frau Lenore, it is safe to assume, could not have received the news with greater despair. She immediately sat down in a corner, with her face to the wall, and burst into tears, almost wailing, for all the world like a Russian peasant woman over the coffin of her husband or son. At first Gemma was so taken aback that she did not even go up to her mother, but stopped dead, standing still like a statue in the middle of the room; Sanin, on the other hand, was so utterly confounded that he was almost afraid of bursting into tears himself! The inconsolable weeping went on for a whole hour—a whole hour! Pantaleone thought it wise to lock the street door of the shop, so that no stranger should come in, for it was still rather early in the day. The old man himself was puzzled; in any case, he did not approve of the haste with which Sanin and Gemma had acted, though he was unwilling to condemn them and was ready to offer them his support in case of need: he disliked Klüber too much! Emilio considered himself to be the intermediary between his friend and his sister, and was almost proud of the fact that it had all turned out so well! He could not for the life of him understand why Frau Lenore was so distraught, and he made up his mind at once that women, even the best of them, suffer from a lack of reasoning power. Sanin was the worst off. Frau Lenore began wailing at the top of her voice and waving him away as soon as he went near her, and it was in vain that he tried, standing at a distance, to say several times in a loud voice: 'I ask you for your daughter's hand!' For Frau Lenore was particularly vexed with herself for having been so blind as not to notice anything! 'If my Giovann' Battista had been alive,' she kept repeating through her tears, 'nothing of the kind would have happened!' 'Good Lord,' thought Sanin, 'what's it all about? Why, it's too damned silly for words!' He did not dare to look at Gemma and she could not summon enough courage to raise her eyes to him. All she did was patiently to look after her mother, who at first pushed her away too. . . .

At last, little by little, the storm subsided. Frau Lenore stopped crying, let Gemma bring her out of the corner where she had ensconced herself, help her to sit down in an armchair by the window and make her drink some water with *fleur d'orange*; she let Sanin — not come near her . . . oh dear, no! — but, at any rate, remain in the room (before, she had kept demanding that he should go away), and did not interrupt him when he spoke. Sanin immediately took advantage of the calm that had set in, and displayed quite an amazing eloquence: he could hardly have expressed his intentions and feelings with such warmth and with such conviction to Gemma herself. Those feelings were most sincere, those intentions were most honourable, like Almaviva's in *The Barber of Seville*. He did not conceal from Frau Lenore nor from himself the disadvantageous side of those intentions; but the disadvantages were merely illusory! It was true that he was a foreigner, that they had only recently met him for the first time, that they did not know anything positive about his person or his means; but he was ready to bring all the necessary proof to show that he was an honest man and far from poor; he would refer them to the most infallible testimony of his fellow-countrymen! He hoped that Gemma would be happy with him and that he would be able to make up to her for the separation from her family! . . . The mention of the separation—the mere word 'separation'—nearly spoilt everything. . . . Frau Lenore became terribly agitated and began trembling violently. . . . Sanin hastened to explain that the separation would only be temporary and that, after all, there might be no separation at all!

Sanin's eloquence was not wasted. Frau Lenore began glancing at him, though still with bitterness and reproach, but no longer with her former abhorrence and anger; then she permitted him to approach her and even to sit down beside her (Gemma was sitting on the other side); then she began reproaching him, not in looks only, but also in words, which meant that her heart was already beginning to be somewhat mollified; she began complaining, and her complaints got quieter and gentler; they alternated with questions addressed to her daughter and to Sanin in turn; then she let him take her hand and did not take it away immediately; then she wept again, but her tears were quite different; then she smiled sadly and expressed her regret at the absence of Giovann' Battista, but for quite a different reason. Another moment passed and both criminals—Sanin and Gemma—were on their knees at her feet and she was laying her hands on their heads in turn; another moment and they were embracing and kissing her, and Emilio, with his face beaming with delight, rushed into the room and also joined the closely united group.

Pantaleone peered into the room, grinned and frowned at one and the same time, and going into the shop unlocked the street door.

30

THE transition from despair to sadness and from sadness to 'quiet resignation' took place pretty rapidly in Frau Lenore; but it did not take long even for this quiet resignation to be transformed into secret contentment which was, however, in every way concealed and checked for the sake of decorum. Frau Lenore had taken a liking to Sanin from the very first day of their acquaintance; having got used to the idea that he would be her son-in-law, she found nothing particularly disagreeable about it, though she did consider it her duty to look hurt or rather worried. Besides, every-thing that had happened during the last few days had been so extraordinary.... One thing on top of another! ... As a practical woman and a mother, Frau Lenore also thought it to be her duty to put all sorts of questions to Sanin; and Sanin who, when he had gone to keep the appointment with Gemma in the morning, had never even remotely considered the possibility of marrying her—though it is true he did not think of anything at the time, but gave himself up entirely to the call of his passion—Sanin entered into his part, the part of a fiancé, with the utmost readiness and, one might even say, with enthusiasm, and answered all the questions willingly, circumstantially, and in full detail. Having satisfied herself that he was a real nobleman by birth and even expressing her surprise that he was not a prince, Frau Lenore assumed a grave air, and 'warned him beforehand' that she would be quite unceremoni-ously frank with him because she was compelled to be so by her sacred duty as a mother! To which Sanin replied that he never expected anything else from her and begged her most earnestly not to spare him!

Then Frau Lenore remarked to him that Herr Klüber (in uttering that name she heaved a faint sigh, tightened her lips and hesitated for a fraction of a second), Herr Klüber, Gemma's ex-fiancé, already had an income of eight thousand guldens and that with every year that sum would rapidly increase, and what, she wanted to know, was Monsieur Sanin's income?

'Eight thousand guldens,' Sanin repeated slowly, 'that's about fifteen thousand roubles in Russian money.... I'm afraid my income is much smaller.... I own a small estate in the province of Tula.... Run efficiently, it might bring in—and, in fact, it ought to bring in—five or six thousand a year ... ought to; and if I joined the civil service, I could easily earn another two thousand. . . .'

'In Russia?' cried Frau Lenore. 'That means that I shall have to part with Gemma, doesn't it?'

'I *could* enter the Russian diplomatic service,' Sanin put in quickly. 'I have certain connections, you see. Then I could get a job abroad. Or else I could do something else—in fact, that would be much better in every respect, I mean I could sell my estate and use the money in some profitable enterprise, for instance, in the improvement of your shop! . . .'

Sanin felt that what he was saying was absurd, but he was seized with a feeling of quite incomprehensible recklessness. He would glance at Gemma, who kept getting up, walking up and down the room and sitting down again as soon as the 'practical' conversation started, he would look at her, and there was nothing he would not do, and he was ready to arrange everything at once in the best possible way, if only she did not worry!

'Herr Klüber also wanted to give me a small sum for the improvement of the shop,' Frau Lenore said, after a slight hesitation.

'Mother! For God's sake, Mother!' cried Gemma in Italian.

'One must discuss these things in good time, my daughter,' Frau Lenore replied to her in the same language.

She turned to Sanin again and began questioning him about Russian marriage laws and whether marriages to Catholic women were forbidden in his country as in Prussia. (In those days, in 1840, all Germany still remembered the quarrel between the Prussian Government and the Archbishop of Cologne over mixed marriages.) But when Frau Lenore heard that by marrying a Russian nobleman, her daughter would become a noblewoman herself, she seemed rather pleased.

'But you have to go to Russia first, haven't you?'

'Why?'

'To get your Emperor's permission, of course!'

Sanin explained to her that that was not at all necessary, but that he might certainly have to go back to Russia for a very short time before his wedding (he uttered those words and his heart contracted painfully, and Gemma, who was looking at him, realized it and blushed and looked thoughtful) and that he would try to take advantage of his stay in his native country to sell his estate. . . . In any case, he would bring back the money they needed.

'I'd also like to ask you to bring me back some good Astrakhan lambskins for a cloak,' said Frau Lenore. 'I hear they are wonderfully good and fabulously cheap there.'

'Certainly, with the greatest of pleasure I'll bring some for you and for Gemma too!' cried Sanin.

'And for me a silver-embroidered morocco cap,' Emilio put in, thrusting his head in from the next room.

'Very well, I'll get it for you, too, and a pair of slippers for Pantaleone.'

'Why talk about such trifles? Why?' observed Frau Lenore. 'We're discussing serious matters now. And another thing,' added the practical lady, 'you talk of selling your estate. But how are you going to do that? You are not going to sell your peasants, too, are you?'

Sanin winced. He recalled that when discussing serfdom with Signora Roselli and her daughter which, as he expressed it, aroused a feeling of the deepest indignation in him, he had assured them again and again that never on any account would he sell his peasants, for he considered such a sale to be immoral.

'I'll try to sell my estate to a man whom I know to be trustworthy,' he said, not without hesitation. 'Or perhaps the peasants themselves will want to buy their freedom.'

'That would be best of all,' Frau Lenore, too, agreed. 'Otherwise, to sell live people ...'

'*Barbari!*' muttered Pantaleone, who also appeared at the door behind Emilio, shaking his quiff, and disappeared.

'That's bad,' thought Sanin, glancing stealthily at Gemma, but she did not seem to have heard his last words. 'Well, never mind!' he thought again.

Their practical talk went on like this almost until dinner-time. In the end Frau Lenore was completely appeased, and already called Sanin by his Christian name, shook her finger affectionately at him and threatened to get her own back on him for his perfidy. She questioned him at length and in great detail about his relations because, as she put it, 'that, too, is very important'. She also asked him to describe the wedding ceremony according to the rites of the Russian Church, and was already admiring Gemma in a white wedding dress with a gold crown on her head.

'You see,' she said with motherly pride, 'she's as beautiful as a queen, and indeed, you won't find a queen like her in the whole world!'

'There's not another Gemma in the world!' Sanin put in enthusiastically.

'Yes, that's why she is Gemma!'

(Gemma, as everyone knows, means a jewel in Italian.)

Gemma rushed up to her mother and began kissing her. ... It seemed as though it were only now that she breathed freely again, and the load that had weighed so heavily on her had dropped from her soul.

As for Sanin, he suddenly felt so happy, his heart was filled with such childlike gaiety at the thought that his dearest dreams, the dreams in which he had so recently indulged in these very rooms, had come true; his whole being was in such a ferment that he went out into the shop at once. He felt that he simply had to serve behind the counter and try to sell something, as he had done a few days earlier. . . . 'I am fully entitled to do so,' he seemed to say to himself, 'for I am one of the family now!'

And he did stand behind the counter and did do some business, that is to say, he sold a pound of sweets to two little girls who came in, giving them two pounds instead of one and charging them half the price.

At dinner he sat beside Gemma and was thus officially acknowledged as her fiancé. Frau Lenore continued her practical deliberations. Emilio kept laughing and pestering Sanin to take him to Russia with him. It was decided that Sanin should leave in a fortnight. Pantaleone alone looked a little glum, so much so that Frau Lenore scolded him. 'And you a second, too!' Pantaleone scowled at her.

Gemma was silent almost all the time, but never before did her face look more beautiful or more radiant. After dinner she called Sanin out into the garden for a minute and, stopping before the seat where she had been sorting out the cherries two days before, said to him:

'Dimitry, don't be angry with me, but I want to remind you again that you must not consider yourself under any obligation . . .'

He did not let her finish. Gemma turned away her face.

'And as for what Mother was saying—remember?—about the difference of our religion—here!'

She snatched the garnet cross, which hung on a thin cord round her neck, gave it a violent pull, broke the cord, and gave him the cross.

'If I am yours, then your religion is mine, too!'

Sanin's eyes were still wet when he returned to the house with Gemma.

By the evening everything was going on as usual. They even played a game of *tresette*.

31

SANIN woke up very early next day. He was in a state of the utmost felicity; but it was not that that prevented him from sleeping; the question, the vital, fateful question of how he could sell his estate as quickly and as profitably as possible disturbed his peace of mind. His head was full of all sorts of plans, but so far nothing definite had emerged. He left the house for a breath of fresh air. He made up his mind that next time he saw Gemma it would be with a plan all ready made, and not otherwise.

What was that figure, rather massive and with thick legs, though quite well-dressed, walking in front of him, swaying from side to side and waddling a little? Where had he seen the back of that head, covered with thick, almost colourless fair hair, that head, which seemed to be planted straight on the shoulders, that soft, fat back, those plump, loose-hanging hands? Could it be Polozov, his old boarding-school classmate whom he had lost sight of for five years now? Sanin overtook the figure walking in front of him and turned round. . . . A broad, yellowish face, small pig's eyes with white lashes and eyebrows, a short, flat nose, full lips, which looked as though they had been glued together, a round, hairless chin—and that expression, sour, torpid and mistrustful—yes indeed: it was he, it was Ippolit Polozov!

'Is it my lucky star again?' flashed across Sanin's mind.

'Polozov! Ippolit Sidorych! Is it you?'

The figure stopped, raised its tiny eyes, waited a little —and, ungluing its lips at last, said in a hoarse falsetto:

'Dimitry Sanin?'

'Yes, the same!' cried Sanin, shaking one of Polozov's hands; arrayed in tight kid gloves of an ashen-grey colour, they hung as lifelessly as before beside his bulging thighs. 'Have you been here long? Where have you come from? Where are you staying?'

'I arrived yesterday from Wiesbaden,' Polozov replied unhurriedly. 'Came here to do some shopping for my wife. Going back to Wiesbaden today.'

'Oh, of course! You're married and, they say, to a very beautiful woman!'

Polozov looked away.

'Yes, so they say.'

Sanin laughed.

'I can see you're just the same, as phlegmatic as you were at school.'

'Why should I change?'

'And they say,' added Sanin with special emphasis on 'say', 'that your wife is very rich.'

'They say that too.'

'Why? Don't you know?'

'You see, my dear Dimitry—er—Pavlovich, isn't it? —yes, Pavlovich! I don't meddle in my wife's affairs!'

'You don't? Not in any of her affairs?'

Polozov again turned his eyes away.

'Not in any, my dear fellow. She minds her own business and I —well, I mind mine.'

'Where are you going now?' asked Sanin.

'Now I'm not going anywhere. I'm standing in the street and talking to you. But after I've finished with you, I'm going back to my hotel and shall have lunch there.'

'You don't mind if I join you, do you?'

'You mean at lunch?'

'Yes.'

'With pleasure. It's much jollier to eat in company. You're not a chatterbox, are you?'

'I don't think so.'

'Well, all right, then.'

Polozov moved on. Sanin walked beside him. And Sanin thought to himself—Polozov's lips were glued together again, he was wheezing and waddling in silence—Sanin thought to himself: how had this dolt succeeded in catching a rich and beautiful wife? He was neither rich, nor clever, nor of a good family himself; at the boarding-school he was considered to be a dull, slow-witted boy, a glutton and a sluggard—and he was nicknamed 'slobberer'. Miracles never cease!

'But if his wife is very rich—I hear she's the

daughter of some tax-farmer—why shouldn't she buy my estate? Though he does say that he doesn't interfere in his wife's affairs, but, surely, you can't possibly believe that! Besides, I'd fix a reasonable, moderate price! Why not try it? Perhaps it's all my lucky star. . . . All right! I'll have a try!'

Polozov took Sanin to one of the best Frankfort hotels in which he was, of course, occupying the best room. Cardboard boxes, bags and parcels were piled on the tables and chairs. . . . 'All purchases, my dear fellow, for Maria Nikolayevna' (that was his wife's name). Polozov sank into an armchair, groaned, 'Oh, the heat!' and undid his tie. Then he rang for the head waiter and ordered a most opulent luncheon with great care. 'And I want my carriage at one o'clock! Do you hear? At one o'clock sharp!'

The head waiter bowed obsequiously and went out cringingly.

Polozov unbuttoned his waistcoat. From the very way in which he raised his eyebrows, puffed, and wrinkled his nose, one could gather that talking would be a very painful business to him and that he was waiting in some alarm to see whether Sanin would make him wag his tongue or whether he would take the trouble to keep the conversation going himself.

Sanin understood his friend's trend of thought, and did not therefore burden him with questions; he confined himself to the most important matters; he learnt that Polozov had spent two years in the army (in an Uhlan regiment! He must have looked a sight in the short tunic!), that he had got married three years before, and had for almost two years now been abroad with his wife, 'who is undergoing some sort of cure in Wiesbaden', and was going to Paris afterwards. For his part, Sanin spoke little of his own past life and his plans;

he went straight to business, that is, he began talking of his intention of selling his estate.

Polozov listened to him in silence, only occasionally glancing at the door through which their lunch was to appear. Lunch did appear at last. The head-waiter, accompanied by two more waiters, brought in several dishes under silver covers.

'Is your estate in the Tula province?' said Polozov, sitting down at the table and tucking a napkin into the collar of his shirt.

'Yes.'

'Yefremov district. . . . I know.'

'You know my Alexeyevka?' asked Sanin, also sitting down at the table.

'Of course I know it.' Polozov stuffed into his mouth a piece of omelette with truffles. 'My wife, Maria Nikolayevna, owns an estate in the neighbourhood. . . . Uncork that bottle, waiter! The land there is quite decent—only your peasants have cut down your woods. Why are you selling it?'

'I want the money, my dear fellow. I'd sell it cheap. Why not buy it? An excellent opportunity.'

Polozov gulped down a glass of wine, wiped his lips with the napkin and again began to chew, slowly and noisily.

'Mmm. . . . Yes,' he said at last. 'I'm afraid I can't afford to buy estates—haven't the money. Pass the butter, please. But my wife may buy it. You talk it over with her. If you don't ask too much, she won't be too particular about it. . . . What asses these Germans are, though! Can't cook fish. And yet what could be simpler? And then they go on talking about uniting their *Vaterland*! Waiter, take away this beastly stuff!'

'But does your wife deal with—er—farming matters herself?' asked Sanin.

'Yes, she does. Now the cutlets are first-class. I can recommend them. I told you that I don't interfere in any of my wife's affairs—and I tell you so again now.'

Polozov continued to eat noisily.

'H'm. But how am I to talk it over with her?'

'Quite simply, my dear fellow. Go to Wiesbaden. It's not far from here. Waiter, haven't you any English mustard? No? Brutes! Only there's no time to be lost. We shall be leaving the day after tomorrow. Let me pour you out a glass of wine: it's wine with a bouquet— not sour slops!'

Polozov's face coloured and grew animated; it only grew animated when he was eating—or drinking.

'I honestly don't know how to manage it,' muttered Sanin.

'But why are you in such a devil of a hurry?'

'Well, that's the trouble—I am in a hurry, you see!'

'Is it a lot of money you want?'

'Yes, a lot. I—how shall I tell you?—you see, I'm— er—thinking of getting married.'

Polozov put down the glass he had already raised to his lips on the table.

'Getting married!' he said, in a voice hoarse with astonishment, and folded his chubby hands on his stomach. 'Soon?'

'Yes—very soon. . . .'

'Your fiancée is in Russia, of course.'

'No, not in Russia.'

'Where is she then?'

'Here in Frankfort.'

'And who is she?'

'A German girl. No, I'm sorry, an Italian. She lives here.'

'Has she any money?'

'No.'

'Then I suppose you must be very much in love with her!'

'What a funny chap you are! Of course I'm very much in love with her.'

'And that's why you want money?'

'Well, yes . . . yes, yes!'

Polozov gulped down his wine, rinsed out his mouth, washed his hands and wiped them carefully on his napkin, took out a cigar and lighted it. Sanin watched him in silence.

'There's only one thing to do,' growled Polozov at last, tossing back his head and blowing out the smoke in a thin ring. 'Go and see my wife. If she wants to, she'll solve your problem in a jiffy.'

'But how can I see her, your wife, I mean? Didn't you say you were leaving the day after tomorrow?'

Polozov closed his eyes.

'I'll tell you what,' he said at last, rolling the cigar with his lips and sighing. 'Go home, pack your things quickly and come back here. I'm leaving at one o'clock, there's plenty of room in my carriage. I'll take you with me. That's the best thing I can suggest. And now I'm going to have a nap. You see, old man, after a meal I simply must have a nap. Nature demands it and — well, and I won't go against it. Don't you disturb me, either.'

Sanin thought it over and — suddenly raised his head: he had made up his mind!

'Well, all right, I agree. Thank you. I'll be here at half-past twelve and we'll go to Wiesbaden together. I hope your wife won't be angry. . . .'

But Polozov was already snoring. He muttered, 'Don't disturb me!' swung his feet to and fro a few times and fell asleep like a baby.

Sanin cast another glance at his massive figure, his

head, his neck, his upturned chin, round as an apple, and raised high—and, going out of the hotel, hastened at once to Roselli's shop. He had first to tell Gemma.

32

HE found her in the shop together with her mother. Frau Lenore was bending down and measuring the space between the windows with a small folding foot-rule. On seeing Sanin, she stood up and greeted him gaily, though not without a certain amount of embarrassment.

'After what you told me yesterday,' she began, 'I've been wondering all the time how to improve our shop. Here, I think, we could put two small cupboards with looking-glass shelves. It's the fashion now, you know. And then——'

'Excellent, excellent,' Sanin interrupted. 'We shall have to think it all over carefully. But come here, I have something to tell you.'

He took Frau Lenore and Gemma by the arm and led them into the other room. Frau Lenore was alarmed and dropped the foot-rule. Gemma was at first alarmed too, but looking more intently at Sanin she was reassured. His face looked worried, it is true, but at the same time it expressed high spirits and determination.

He asked the two women to sit down and, standing before them, waving his hands about and ruffling his hair, he told them everything: his meeting with Polozov, the proposed journey to Wiesbaden, and the chance of selling his estate.

'Imagine my luck!' he exclaimed at last. 'The whole business has taken such a turn that I may not have to go to Russia at all! And we can have our wedding much earlier than I thought!'

'When have you got to go?' asked Gemma.

'Today, in an hour. My friend has hired a carriage and he's going to take me there.'

'You will write to us, won't you?'

'As soon as I've talked things over with that woman!'

'That woman, you say, is very rich?' asked the practical Frau Lenore.

'Extremely! Her father was a millionaire and he left everything to her.'

'Everything? To her alone? Well, that is lucky for you! Only, mind, don't sell your estate too cheaply! Be sensible and firm. Do not let yourself be carried away! I understand how anxious you must be to become Gemma's husband as soon as possible—but prudence before everything! Don't forget the more you get for your estate, the more there will be for you and Gemma and for your children.'

Gemma turned away and Sanin again started waving his arms about.

'You may count on my prudence, Frau Lenore! I won't even bother to bargain. . . . I'll tell her the price

I want for it: if she agrees—all right, if not—I'll do without her.'

'Do you know her—this woman?' asked Gemma.

'I've never seen her in my life.'

'And when will you return?'

'If our business falls through, the day after to-morrow; if it turns out well, I may have to stay there a day or two. In any event, I won't stay a minute longer than necessary. For I am leaving my heart here! However, I'm afraid I've been forgetting the time talking to you. You see, I have got to dash back to my hotel before leaving. Give me your hand for luck, Frau Lenore—it's an old Russian custom!'

'The right or the left?'

'The left—nearer the heart. I'll come back the day after tomorrow—with my shield or on it! Something tells me I'll return a conqueror! Goodbye, my dears.'

He embraced and kissed Frau Lenore and asked Gemma to follow him into her room—for a minute, as he had to tell her something of importance. . . . He simply wanted to say goodbye to her in private. Frau Lenore realized that and she was not curious to find out what the important thing was. . . .

Sanin had never been in Gemma's room before. All the magic of love, all its fire and rapture, and sweet terror—blazed up in him and burst into his soul as soon as he stepped over the forbidden threshold. . . . He cast a tender glance round the room, fell at the feet of his beloved and pressed his face against her waist.

'You're mine, aren't you?' she whispered. 'You'll come back soon?'

'I'm yours—I'll come back,' he kept repeating breathlessly.

'I'll be waiting for you, my darling!'

A few moments later Sanin was running along the

street to his hotel. He did not even notice that Pantaleone, all dishevelled, had rushed out of the shop after him. He was shouting something to him and was shaking his raised fist, as though threatening him.

*　　*　　*

Exactly at a quarter to one Sanin appeared at Polozov's hotel. The carriage, drawn by four horses, was already standing at the hotel gates. On seeing Sanin, Polozov merely said, 'Oh, so you've made up your mind?' and, putting on his hat, cloak and goloshes and stopping up his ears with cotton-wool, though it was summer, walked out on to the front steps. The waiters, at his directions, put all his numerous purchases inside the carriage, surrounded his seat with silk cushions, bags and little parcels, put at his feet a hamper of provisions and tied his trunk on the box. Polozov tipped everybody generously, and supported very respectfully from behind by the obliging doorkeeper, he climbed groaning into the carriage, settled himself comfortably, carefully patted the cushions round him, selected a cigar and lit it, and only then beckoned to Sanin as if to say: 'Get in you, too!' Sanin sat down beside him. Polozov ordered the doorkeeper to tell the postillion to drive carefully if he wanted a tip; the footboards crashed, the doors slammed, the carriage rolled off.

33

FROM Frankfort to Wiesbaden is now less than an
hour's journey by rail; in those days the express post
took three hours. Horses were changed five times. Polozov either dozed or just swayed from side to side, a
cigar between his teeth, and talked very little; he did
not once look out of the window: he was not interested
in picturesque views and even declared that nature
would be 'the death of me!' Sanin, too, was silent; he
did not admire the scenery either: he had other things
on his mind. He gave himself up entirely to his
thoughts and memories. At the stations Polozov was
meticulous in paying his fare, making a note of the time
by looking at his watch and tipping the postillions—
sometimes more, sometimes less, all according to their
zeal. Halfway to Wiesbaden, he took two oranges out
of the hamper and, selecting the better one, offered the
other to Sanin. Sanin looked intently at his fellow-
traveller and suddenly burst out laughing.

'What are you laughing at?' Polozov asked,
carefully peeling his orange with his stubby white
nails.

'What am I laughing at?' Sanin repeated. 'Why, at
this journey of mine with you.'

'What about it?' asked Polozov, placing into his

mouth one of those longitudinal sections into which the flesh of an orange is divided.

'Well, it's rather strange, isn't it? Yesterday, I must confess, I thought of you as little as of the Emperor of China, and today I am driving with you to sell my estate to your wife, of whom I haven't the slightest idea, either.'

'All sorts of things happen in this world,' replied Polozov. 'Live a little longer and you'll see plenty. For instance, can you imagine me riding up as an orderly officer? I did, though. And the Grand Duke Mikhail Pavlovich gave the order: "Trot! Let him trot, that fat cornet! Trot faster!"'

Sanin scratched himself behind his ear. 'Tell me, please,' he said, 'what is your wife like? I mean, what sort of character has she got? You see, I have to know that.'

'It's all very well for him to give the order "Trot!"' Polozov went on with sudden vehemence. 'But what about me? What do you think I felt? Well, so I said to myself, "You can take your honours and epaulettes—to hell with them!" Oh yes . . . you asked about my wife, didn't you? Well, what about my wife? She's a human being, like the rest of us. Don't get her back up —she doesn't like it. The main thing is—talk a lot so that she has something to laugh at. Tell her about your love affair, but—er—make it amusing, you understand?'

'Amusing? What do you mean?'

'Why, of course. Didn't you tell me that you were in love and wanted to get married? Well, describe it all to her.'

Sanin was offended.

'What do you find so amusing about that?'

Polozov just rolled his eyes. The juice from the orange trickled down his chin.

'Did your wife send you to Frankfort to do her shopping?' asked Sanin, after a short pause.

'Yes, she did.'

'What sort of shopping?'

'Oh, some toys.'

'Toys? You haven't any children, have you?'

Polozov shrank back from Sanin.

'Good Lord! Why should I have children? I meant female *colifichets*. . . . Finery, toilet articles.'

'Do you know anything about them?'

'I do.'

'Why, then, did you tell me that you didn't interfere in your wife's affairs?'

'I don't. This has nothing to do with her affairs. I do it from boredom. There's nothing wrong about that, is there? Besides, my wife trusts my taste. I'm jolly good at bargaining, too!'

Polozov was beginning to talk jerkily. He was getting tired.

'Is your wife very rich?'

'She's rich all right. But mostly for herself.'

'I don't think you have anything to complain about, have you?'

'Well, I *am* her husband, aren't I? Why shouldn't I damn well make use of her? And I'm jolly useful to her, too! She's lucky to have got me! I don't make a fuss!'

Polozov wiped his face with a silk handkerchief and blew out his breath noisily: 'For God's sake,' he seemed to say, 'have pity on me! Don't make me utter another word. You see how hard it is for me.'

Sanin left him in peace, and sank into thought once more.

*　　*　　*

The hotel in Wiesbaden, before which the carriage stopped, certainly looked like a palace. Bells started ringing at once in its innermost recesses; a commotion arose, people began rushing to and fro all over the place; handsome men in black frock-coats came skipping to the main entrance; the doorkeeper, covered in gold braid from head to foot, flung open the carriage doors.

Polozov got out of the carriage like some conquering hero and began mounting the carpeted and scented staircase. A man, also immaculately dressed, but with a Russian face, rushed up to him: it was his valet. Polozov told him that in future he would always take him on his journeys with him, for in Frankfort the night before he, Polozov, had been left for the night without hot water! The valet's face registered horror as he bent down deftly and took off his master's goloshes.

'Is Maria Nikolayevna at home?' asked Polozov.

'Yes, sir. She's dressing, sir. She had dinner at Countess Lassunsky's.'

'Oh, at her place! Wait! There are the things in the carriage. Take everything out yourself and bring them in. And you, Sanin,' added Polozov, 'book yourself a room and come up in three-quarters of an hour. We'll dine together.'

Polozov waddled off, while Sanin booked a room that was not too expensive and, after tidying himself and resting a little, went to the enormous suite of rooms occupied by his Serenity (*Durchlaucht*) Prince von Polozov.

He found the 'prince' enthroned in a most magnificent velvet armchair in the middle of a most resplendent drawing-room. Sanin's phlegmatic friend had had time to have a bath and to array himself in a most expensive satin dressing-gown; on his head he wore a crimson fez. Sanin went up to him and examined him carefully for some time. Polozov sat as motionless as an idol; he did not even turn his face towards him, he did not even raise an eyebrow, did not utter a sound. It was, indeed, a majestic sight! After having admired him for a minute or two, Sanin was about to say something, to break this sacred silence, when suddenly the door of the adjoining room was opened and there appeared in the doorway a young and beautiful woman in a white silk dress trimmed with black lace and with diamonds on her fingers and neck—Maria Nikolayevna Polozov herself. Her thick, brown hair fell on either side of her head—plaited, but not gathered up on top.

34

'Oh, I'm so sorry,' she said, with a half-embarrassed, half-ironic smile, snatching up at once the end of a plait and fixing her large, bright grey eyes on Sanin. 'I didn't realize that you were here already.'

'Sanin, Dimitry Pavlovich, my childhood friend,' said Polozov, without, as before, turning towards him and without getting up, but pointing at him with a finger.

'Yes—I know, you've already told me, dear. Very pleased to meet you. But I wanted to ask you to do something for me, Ippolit. . . . My maid is so stupid today. . . .'

'Do up your hair?'

'Yes, please. I'm sorry,' repeated Maria Nikolayevna with the same smile, nodded to Sanin and, turning round quickly, disappeared behind the door, leaving behind her a fleeting but agreeable impression of an exquisite neck, marvellous shoulders and a marvellous figure.

Polozov got up and, waddling cumbrously, went out of the same door.

Sanin did not doubt for a moment that Maria Nikolayevna knew perfectly well of his presence in 'Prince Polozov's' drawing-room; the whole idea of her appearance was to show off her hair, which really was beautiful. Sanin was inwardly even glad of this piece of vanity on the part of Madame Polozov—'If,' he reflected, 'you wanted to surprise me, to show off before me, then perhaps—who knows?—you may show yourself amenable also about the price of my estate!' His heart was so full of Gemma that all other women were absolutely of no significance to him: he hardly noticed them; and this time, too, all he thought was: 'Yes, it's true what they told me: milady is certainly a bit of all right!'

But had he not been in such an exceptional frame of mind, he would probably have expressed himself differently: Maria Nikolayevna Polozov, née Kolyshkin, was a very remarkable woman. Not that she was a perfect beauty: traces of her plebeian origin could be quite clearly detected in her. Her forehead was low, her nose a trifle too fleshy and turned up; she could boast neither delicacy of skin nor elegance of arms and feet—but what did it all matter? Anyone meeting her would have stopped dead not before what Pushkin called 'the holy shrine of beauty', but before the fascinating and overwhelmingly powerful half-Russian, half-gipsy body of a woman in the full bloom of youth!

But Gemma's image protected Sanin like the triple armour of which poets sing.

Ten minutes later Maria Nikolayevna appeared again in the company of her husband. She went up to Sanin—and her walk was such that some eccentrics in those, alas, already far-off days lost their heads from the way she walked alone. 'When this woman comes up to you, it is as though she were carrying all your life's happiness towards you,' one of them used to say. She went up to Sanin and, holding out her hand to him, said in her caressing and seemingly restrained voice in Russian: 'You will wait for me, won't you? I'll be back soon.'

Sanin bowed respectfully, while Maria Nikolayevna was disappearing behind the curtain of the door and, as she disappeared, she looked over one shoulder again and again smiled and again left behind her the same agreeable impression.

When she smiled, not one or two, but three dimples appeared on each cheek, and her eyes smiled more than her lips, more than her long, delicious, scarlet lips with two tiny moles on the left side of them.

Polozov lurched into the room and once more settled himself in the armchair. He was as silent as ever; but from time to time a strange grin played over his colourless and already wrinkled cheeks.

He looked old, though he was only three years older than Sanin.

The dinner with which he regaled his guest would

of course have satisfied the most fastidious gourmet, but to Sanin it seemed endless and quite insupportable! Polozov ate slowly, 'with feeling, judgment and deliberation', bending attentively over his plate, sniffing at almost every morsel; first he rinsed his mouth with wine, then he swallowed it, and then he smacked his lips. . . . Over the roast meat he suddenly began to talk—but about what? About merino sheep, of which he intended to order a whole flock—and in such detail, with such tenderness, using only the most caressing names for them. After drinking a scalding-hot cup of coffee (he had several times reminded the waiter in a tearful, irritable voice that the evening before he had been served with coffee that was cold, cold as ice!), and biting off the end of a Havana cigar with his crooked yellow teeth he, as was his custom, dozed off, to Sanin's great delight. Sanin started walking noiselessly up and down the room on the thick carpet, dreaming of the time when he would live with Gemma and wondering what news he would bring back to her. Polozov, however, woke up, as he remarked himself, earlier than usual—he had slept only an hour and a half—and after drinking a glass of iced soda water and swallowing about eight spoonsful of jam, Russian jam, which his valet had brought him in a dark-green genuine 'Kiev' jar, without which, he declared, he could not live, he glared with his swollen eyes at Sanin and asked him if he would like to have a game of 'fools' with him. Sanin agreed gladly; he was afraid that Polozov might start talking again about sweet little lambs, darling yearling ewes and lovely sheep with fat tails. The host and his guest both went into the drawing-room, the waiter brought in a pack of cards and the game began, not for money, of course.

At that innocent pastime they were discovered by

Maria Nikolayevna on her return from the Countess Lassunsky's.

She laughed loudly as soon as she entered the room and saw the cards and the open card-table. Sanin jumped up from his place, but she cried:

'Sit down, please, and go on playing. I'm going to change and I'll come back to you,' and she disappeared again with a swish of her dress and pulling off her gloves as she went.

And, indeed, she did return soon. She had changed her smart dress for a wide lilac silk gown with loose hanging sleeves; round her waist was a thick, twisted cord. She sat down beside her husband and, waiting till he was out for a 'fool', said to him: 'Well, dumpling, that's enough!' (At the word 'dumpling' Sanin looked up at her in astonishment, but she smiled gaily, responding to his glance by a glance and showing all the dimples in her cheeks.) 'Enough! I can see that you are sleepy. Kiss my hand and off to bed with you! Monsieur Sanin and I will have a talk together alone.'

'I am not at all sleepy,' said Polozov, getting up heavily from his chair. 'But I don't mind going off to bed and kissing your hand.'

She held out her hand to him, smiling all the time, and looking at Sanin.

Polozov, too, looked at him and, without taking leave, left the room.

'Well, tell me, tell me,' said Maria Nikolayevna animatedly, putting both her bare elbows on the table and impatiently tapping the nails of one hand on the nails of the other. 'Is it true what I hear about your getting married?'

Having uttered these words, Maria Nikolayevna even bent her head on one side a little in order to gaze more intently and more piercingly into Sanin's eyes.

35

MADAME POLOZOV's free-and-easy manner would at first probably have embarrassed Sanin—though he was no greenhorn and had had some experience of the world—had he not again regarded this very presumption and familiarity as a good augury for the success of his undertaking. 'Let's humour the caprices of this rich madam,' he said to himself, and answered her as unconstrainedly as she had questioned him.

'Yes, I'm getting married.'

'To whom? A foreigner?'

'Yes.'

'You only met her recently, didn't you? Where was it? In Frankfort?'

'Yes.'

'And who is she? May I know?'

'You may. She is the daughter of a confectioner.'

Maria Nikolayevna opened her eyes wide and raised her eyebrows.

'Why,' she said in a drawn-out voice, 'this is charming! It's wonderful! And I thought that such young men as you no longer existed. A confectioner's daughter!'

'I see that surprises you,' Sanin observed, not without a touch of dignity. 'But, in the first place, I have none of these prejudices. . . .'

'*In the first place*, it does not surprise me in the least,' Maria Nikolayevna interrupted him. 'I have no prejudices, either. I am the daughter of a peasant myself. Well? I've got you there, haven't I? What surprises and pleases me is that here's a man who is not afraid to love. You do love her, don't you?'

'Yes.'

'Is she very pretty?'

The last question made Sanin wince a little. . . . However, it was too late to draw back.

'I expect you know,' he said, 'that every man who is in love thinks the face of the girl he loves prettier than any other; but my fiancée really is a beauty.'

'Is she? What kind of a beauty? Italian? Antique?'

'Yes, she has very regular features.'

'You haven't got her portrait, have you?'

'No.' (In those days there were no photographs. Daguerreotypes were only just beginning to be popular.)

'What's her name?'

'Gemma.'

'And yours?'

'Dimitry.'

'Your patronymic?'

'Pavlovich.'

'You know,' said Maria Nikolayevna, still in the same languorous voice, 'I like you very much. I think you must be a nice person. Give me your hand. Let's be friends.'

She pressed his hand firmly with her beautiful, strong white fingers. Her hand was slightly smaller than his, but much warmer, smoother, softer and more vital.

'Only do you know what occurs to me?'

'What?'

135

'You won't be angry with me? No? You say she is your fiancée. But was that—was that absolutely necessary?'

Sanin frowned.

'I don't understand you.'

Maria Nikolayevna laughed very softly and, with a toss of her head, threw back the hair that fell over her cheeks.

'He really is delightful,' she murmured, half-thoughtfully, half-absently. 'A perfect knight! After that one can't believe the people who say that idealists don't exist any more, can one?'

Maria Nikolayevna spoke all the time in Russian, a surprisingly pure Moscow Russian, as the people and not the nobility speak the language.

'I suppose you were brought up at home in a God-fearing, patriarchal family, weren't you?' she asked. 'What province are you from?'

'Tula.'

'Well, in that case, we're neighbours. My father . . . You know, of course, who my father was?'

'Yes, I know.'

'He was born in Tula. . . . He was a native of Tula. Right.' (Maria Nikolayevna deliberately pronounced the word as artisans do: Roit!) 'Well, then, to business.'

'To business? I'm sorry, I don't quite follow you . . .'

Maria Nikolayevna screwed up her eyes.

'Why, what did you come here for?' (When she screwed up her eyes, there was a very caressing and a slightly ironic look in them; but when she opened them wide, something evil, something menacing, came into their bright, almost cold brilliance. Her thick, slightly beetling, truly sable-like eyebrows made her eyes look quite extraordinarily beautiful.) 'You want me to buy your estate, don't you? You want money for your wedding, don't you? Isn't that so?'

'Yes.'

'And do you want much?'

'I should be satisfied with a few thousand francs at first. Your husband knows my estate. You could consult him. I would accept quite a moderate price.'

Maria Nikolayevna shook her head from side to side.

'*In the first place*,' she began slowly, tapping the lapel of Sanin's coat with the tips of her fingers, 'I am not in the habit of consulting my husband, except perhaps about my dresses—he is excellent at that; and *secondly*, why do you say that you would accept a moderate price? I don't want to take advantage of your being very much in love just now and ready to make any sacrifices. . . . I won't accept any sacrifices from you. . . . Good heavens, instead of encouraging your —how shall I put it?—honourable feelings, do you expect me to fleece you? I'm afraid I'm not that kind of person. Whenever necessary, I can be ruthless with people, only not in that way.'

Sanin could not for the life of him say whether she was laughing at him or speaking seriously. All he thought was: 'Why, one must mind one's step with you!'

A servant came in carrying a Russian *samovar*, a tea service, cream, biscuits, etc., on a large tray; he put all these delights on the table between Sanin and Madame Polozov, and left the room.

She poured him out a cup of tea.

'You don't mind my fingers, do you?' she asked, putting the sugar into his cup with her fingers, even though the sugar-tongs were close at hand.

'Good Lord, from such a lovely hand . . .'

He did not finish the sentence and nearly choked as he tried to gulp down his tea, while she looked attentively and serenely at him.

'The reason why I mentioned a moderate price for my estate,' he went on, 'was because I thought that as you are abroad now I can hardly expect you to have a lot of ready cash and, as a matter of fact, I can't help feeling myself that the sale or—er—purchase of an estate under such conditions is something exceptional, and I ought to take that into consideration.'

Sanin got flustered and confused, while Maria Nikolayevna quietly leaned back in her armchair, folded her hands and looked at him with the same attentive and serene eyes. At last he fell silent.

'Please, go on, go on,' she said, as though coming to his aid. 'I'm listening to you, I like listening to you: please, go on!'

Sanin began to describe his estate, how many acres it contained, where it was situated, what its arable land, pasture and forests were like, and what profits one could make from it . . . he even mentioned the picturesque situation of the manor house; while Maria Nikolayevna kept on looking and looking at him more and more serenely and more and more intently, her lips moving faintly, without smiling: she was biting them. At last he felt awkward; he fell silent for a second time.

'Dimitry Pavlovich,' began Maria Nikolayevna and fell into thought. 'Dimitry Pavlovich,' she repeated, 'you know I'm quite sure that the purchase of your estate will turn out to be a very profitable transaction for me and that we'll come to terms, but you must give me—two days—yes, two days' grace. You don't mind parting from your fiancée for two days, do you? I won't keep you longer against your will, I give you my word of honour. But if you need five or six thousand francs now, I shall be very pleased to lend them to you—and we'll settle later.'

Sanin got up.

'I must thank you, Maria Nikolayevna, for your most kind readiness to be of service to a man who is almost completely unknown to you. . . . But if you insist, I'd rather wait for your decision about my estate—I'll stay here two days.'

'Yes, I do insist. But will it make you very unhappy? Very? Tell me.'

'I love my fiancée, and I don't find separation from her easy.'

'Oh, you're a wonderful man!' Maria Nikolayevna said with a sigh. 'I promise not to keep you hanging about too long. Are you going?'

'It's late,' observed Sanin.

'And you have to have a rest after your journey and your game of "fools" with my husband. Tell me, are you a great friend of my husband's?'

'We were at the same boarding-school.'

'And was he the same then?'

'The same as what?' asked Sanin.

Maria Nikolayevna burst out laughing and laughed till she was red in the face, then she put her handkerchief to her lips, got up from her chair, and swaying as if she were very tired, went up to Sanin and held out her hand to him.

He took his leave and went to the door.

'Please, come early tomorrow, do you hear?' she called after him.

He looked back as he was going out of the room and saw that she had sunk into the armchair again and flung both her arms behind her head. The wide sleeves of her gown rolled back almost to her shoulders—and it was impossible not to admit that the pose of her arms, that her whole figure, was ravishingly beautiful.

36

THE lamp in Sanin's room was burning long after midnight. He was sitting at the table and writing to 'his Gemma'. He told her everything; he described the Polozovs—husband and wife—though he expatiated more on his own feelings and finished by fixing a meeting with her in three days!!! (with three exclamation marks). He posted the letter early next morning and went for a walk in the Kurhaus Gardens, where the band was already playing. There were still very few people about; he stood before the bandstand, listened to a potpourri from *Robert le Diable* and, after drinking a cup of coffee, walked along a secluded avenue, where he sat down on a bench and fell into thought.

The handle of a parasol gave him a few quick and rather powerful raps on the shoulder. He gave a start. ... Before him, in a light, greyish-green Barèges dress, a white tulle hat and suède gloves, stood Maria Nikolayevna, looking as fresh and rosy as a summer morning, though the languor of serene and tranquil sleep had not yet vanished from her movements and her eyes.

'Good morning,' she said. 'I sent for you this morning but you'd already gone out. I've just had my second glass—they're making me drink the waters here, you know, goodness only knows why—me of all people not in good health? And so I have to walk for a whole hour now. Would you like to accompany me? We shall have some coffee afterwards.'

'I've had some already,' said Sanin, getting up, 'but I shall be very glad to walk with you.'

'Well, give me your arm. . . . Don't be afraid, your fiancée isn't here—she won't see you.'

Sanin smiled sheepishly. He had an unpleasant feeling every time Maria Nikolayevna mentioned Gemma. However, he bent forward hastily and obediently. . . . Maria Nikolayevna's hand dropped slowly and softly on to his arm, slipped into it and seemed to cling to it.

'Come along—this way, please,' she said, opening her parasol and holding it over her shoulder, 'I'm quite at home in this park: I'll take you to the best places. And, you know' (she often used those two words), 'don't let's talk about that sale now; we shall discuss it thoroughly after lunch. I think you ought to tell me about yourself now, so that I—er—should know whom I'm dealing with. After that, if you wish, I'll tell you all about myself. Do you agree?'

'But what could you find so interesting about . . .'

'Wait, wait. I'm afraid you didn't understand me properly. I don't want to flirt with you.' Maria Nikolayevna shrugged her shoulders. 'He's got a fiancée like an ancient statue, and me flirt with him! But you've got something to sell and I'm a business woman. I'd like to know what kind of goods you've got. Well, show me them—what are they like? I must know not only what I'm buying but who I'm buying from. That was my father's rule. Well, begin. . . . Well, tell me if not about your childhood, then how long you've been abroad. And where have you been till now? Only don't walk so fast, please, we're in no hurry.'

'I came here from Italy where I spent several months.'

'I can see you feel a special attraction to everything Italian. It is strange that it was not *there* that you fell in love. . . . Do you like art? Pictures? Or do you like music more?'

'I like art. . . . I like everything beautiful.'

'And music?'

'And music, too.'

'And I don't like music at all. I only like Russian songs—and that, too, only in a Russian village, and only in the spring—with dancing, you know. . . . Red shirts, strings of beads round girls' heads, young grass in the meadows, the smell of smoke—wonderful! But we were not talking about me. Come on, speak, tell me. . . .'

Maria Nikolayevna walked along, but kept looking at Sanin every now and then. She was tall—her face was almost level with his face.

He began telling her all about himself—at first reluctantly and unskilfully, but soon he was talking quite freely, chattering away, in fact. Maria Nikolayevna was a good listener; besides, she seemed to be so frank herself that others could not help being frank with her. She possessed that great gift of 'making you feel at home'—*le terrible don de la familiarité* Cardinal de Retz speaks of. Sanin told her of his travels, his life in Petersburg, his youth. . . . Had Maria Nikolayevna been a society woman with refined manners, he would never have let himself go like that; but she spoke of herself as 'a good fellow' who could not bear any sort of ceremony herself; that was how she described herself to Sanin. And at the same time there was something cat-like about the way that 'good fellow' walked beside him, brushing herself up against him a little and peering into his face; and this 'good fellow' walked in the shape of a young feminine creature who simply

142

exuded the sort of exciting, soft and fiery allure with which only Slav natures can hold us men, poor, weak sinners that we are, in bondage—and only some of them—those which are not of pure but of the right sort of mixed blood!

Sanin's walk with Maria Nikolayevna, Sanin's talk with Maria Nikolayevna, lasted over an hour. And not once did they stop—they kept on walking and walking along the endless avenues of the park, now going up a hill and admiring the view as they went, and now going down into a valley and becoming hidden in the thick shadows—and all the time arm-in-arm. At times Sanin was even annoyed: he had never walked so long with Gemma, his darling Gemma—and here this rich woman had taken possession of him and there was nothing he could do about it!

'You're not tired, are you?' he asked her more than once.

'I never get tired,' she replied.

From time to time they met people who were also taking a walk in the park; almost all of them bowed to her—some respectfully, others even obsequiously. To one of them, a rather handsome, smartly dressed dark man, she called from a distance in an excellent Parisian accent: '*Comte, vous savez, il ne faut pas venir me voir — ni aujourd'hui, ni demain.*' The man took off his hat in silence and made a low bow.

'Who's that?' asked Sanin, out of the bad habit 'of asking questions out of curiosity'—a bad habit peculiar to all Russians.

'That one? A stupid little Frenchman—there are lots of them here. . . . Another of my admirers. . . . However, it's time we had some coffee. Let's go home. I expect you must be hungry by this time. My better half must have opened his peepers by now!'

'Better half! Opened his peepers!!' Sanin repeated to himself. 'And speaks excellent French! What an extraordinary woman!'

* * *

Maria Nikolayevna was not mistaken. When she and Sanin returned to the hotel, her 'better half' or 'dumpling' was already sitting with the inevitable fez on his head before a table laid for lunch.

'I've been waiting for you!' he cried, making a wry face. 'I was going to have coffee without you.'

'Never mind, never mind,' Maria Nikolayevna replied gaily. 'You are cross? That's good for you. You'd turn into a statue otherwise. Look, I've brought you a visitor. Quick, ring! Let's have coffee—the best coffee in the world—in Saxony cups, on a snow-white tablecloth!'

She threw off her hat and gloves and clapped her hands.

Polozov gave her a sidelong glance.

'What makes you so mettlesome today?' he said, in an undertone.

'It's none of your business, sir! Ring the bell! Dimitry Pavlovich, do sit down—and have some coffee for the second time! Oh, what fun it is to give orders! There is no greater pleasure in the world!'

'When one's orders are carried out,' her husband muttered again.

'Yes, indeed, when they're carried out! That's why I'm so happy! Especially with you. Isn't that so, dumpling? Ah, here's the coffee.'

There was also a playbill on the huge tray which the waiter had brought in. Maria Nikolayevna snatched it up at once.

'A drama!' she said with indignation. 'A German

drama! Oh well, it's better than a German comedy, I suppose. Order a box for me—*baignoire*—or no—better the *Fremden-loge*,' she addressed the waiter: 'do you hear: the *Fremden-loge*!'

'But what if the *Fremden-loge* has already been taken by his excellency the Mayor (*seine Excellenz der Herr Stadt-Direktor*)?' the waiter made bold to object.

'Give his excellency ten thalers, but make sure I get the box! Do you hear?'

The waiter bowed his head humbly and sadly.

'You will go to the theatre with me, won't you, Monsieur Sanin? German actors are awful, but you will come, won't you? You will! How kind of you! Dumpling, I'm sorry, but you can't come!'

'Whatever you say,' said Polozov into the cup he had raised to his lips.

'Yes, I think you'd better stay here. You always go to sleep in the theatre, and you don't understand German very well. . . . I'll tell you what you'd better do: write an answer to my agent—about our flour-mill— remember?—about our flour-mill, about the grinding of the peasants' corn. Tell him, I don't want to, I don't want to and I don't want to! There's occupation for you for the whole evening. . . .'

'All right,' observed Polozov.

'Well, that's settled then. You're a clever boy. And now, gentlemen, since we've been talking about my agent, let's discuss our chief business. As soon as the waiter clears the table, you will tell us about your estate, what it's like, how much you want for it, what kind of deposit you'd like—in short, everything!' ('At last, thank God!' Sanin thought.)

'You have told me something about it already— given me a wonderful description of your garden—but "dumpling" was not present, was he? Let him hear it too—he may mutter something under his breath about it! I'm delighted to think that I can help you to get married. I did promise you to deal with your business after lunch, didn't I? I always keep my promises, don't I, darling?'

Polozov rubbed his face with his hand.

'What's true is true: you don't deceive anyone.'

'Never! And I never will deceive anyone. Well, Monsieur Sanin, state your case, as we say in the senate.'

37

SANIN began to 'state his case', that is to say, to describe his estate a second time, but no longer referring to the beauties of nature and from time to time appealing to Polozov for a confirmation of the 'facts and figures' he had quoted. But Polozov merely grunted and shook his head, whether in approval or not, the devil would have found it hard to say. Still, Maria Nikolayevna did not really need his aid. She revealed such commercial and financial abilities that all Sanin could do was to stare at her in amazement. She had a most perfect knowledge of all the minutest details of farming, she asked about everything and took everything into consideration; her every word was to the point, she dotted every 'i'. Sanin had not expected such an examination. And this examination went on for fully an hour and a half. Sanin experienced all the sensations of a defendant, sitting on a narrow bench in front of a severe and shrewd judge. 'Why,' he whispered dully to himself, 'this is a cross-examination!' Maria Nikolayevna kept smiling slyly all the time, just as though she were joking: but that did not make Sanin feel any better; and when in the course of the 'cross-examination' it came out that he was not quite clear about the meaning of the words 'reallotment' and 'tillage', he came out all over in a cold sweat.

'Well, all right,' Maria Nikolayevna decided at last. 'I have a very good idea of your estate now—as good as you have. What price will you ask for a peasant?' (At that time the price of estates was, of course, determined by the number of peasants.)

'Well, I—I think that I couldn't possibly take less than five hundred roubles,' Sanin brought out with difficulty. (Oh, Pantaleone, Pantaleone, where are you? This is when you should have exclaimed again: *Barbari!*)

Maria Nikolayevna looked upwards as though thinking it over.

'Well,' she said at last, 'the price seems fair enough to me. But I've stipulated for two days to make up my mind and you will have to wait till tomorrow. I expect we shall come to an agreement about the price, and you will then tell me what deposit you want. And now *basta cosi!*' she put in quickly, noticing that Sanin was about to make some objection. 'We've wasted enough time on filthy lucre—*à demain les affaires!* You know,

I'm going to let you go now' (she looked at the enamel watch she wore in her belt) 'till three o'clock. . . . I must let you have some rest, mustn't I? Go and try your luck at the roulette.'

'I never gamble,' observed Sanin.

'Don't you really? Why, you're perfection itself. Still, I don't gamble, either. It's stupid to throw money away. But I think you ought to go to the casino and look at the faces of the people there. Very amusing some of them are. There's an old woman there with a *ferronnière* and a moustache—delightful! There's one of our Russian princes there, too—also a fine one. A majestic figure, an aquiline nose, but every time he puts down a thaler, he crosses himself stealthily under his waistcoat. Read the papers, take a walk—in short, do what you like. But at three o'clock I shall be expecting you—*de pied ferme*. We'll have to have dinner a little earlier. These ridiculous Germans start their performances at half-past six.' She held out her hand. '*Sans rancune, n'est-ce pas?*'

'Good heavens, why should I be vexed with you?'

'Why? Because I've been tormenting you. You wait, this is nothing to what I shall do to you,' she added, screwing up her eyes, and all her dimples appeared all at once on her flushed cheeks. '*Au revoir!*'

Sanin bowed and went out. There was a burst of merry laughter behind him, and in the looking-glass he was passing at that moment the following scene was reflected: Maria Nikolayevna had pulled her husband's fez over his eyes and he was struggling helplessly with both hands.

38

O h, what a deep sigh of relief Sanin heaved when he found himself again in his room! No doubt about it: Maria Nikolayevna had spoken the truth—he needed a rest, a rest from all these new acquaintances, shocks, conversations, from those poisonous fumes that had crept into his head, into his soul, from that unanticipated and unsought intimacy with a woman who was so alien to him! And when was it all happening? Almost the day after he had found out that Gemma loved him, after he had become engaged to her! Why, it was sacrilege! A thousand times in his thoughts he asked his pure, chaste dove to forgive him, though he could not really blame himself for anything; a thousand times he kissed the little cross she had given him. If he had had no hope of bringing the business that had brought him to Wiesbaden to a speedy and successful conclusion, he would have rushed back at once to dear old Frankfort, to that dear house which had now become his second home, to her, to throw himself at her dear feet. . . . But he could do nothing about it! He had to drain the cup to the dregs, he had to dress, go to dinner and from there to the theatre. . . . If only she would let him go tomorrow as early as possible!

There was one more thing that embarrassed him, that angered him: he was thinking with love, with deep emotion, with gratitude and rapture of Gemma, of their life together, of the happiness that awaited him in the future—and yet this strange woman, this Madame Polozov floated—no! not floated—stuck—it was thus that Sanin expressed it with special vindictiveness— *stuck* before his eyes, and he could not rid himself of her image, he could not help hearing her voice, recalling her words, he could not help being aware even of that special scent, delicate, fresh and penetrating, like the scent of yellow lilies, that came from her clothes. That rich woman was quite obviously making a fool of him, flattering and coaxing him in every possible way. . . . Why? What was she after? Was it just the whim of a spoilt, rich and most likely immoral woman? And that husband of hers? What sort of creature was he? What were his relations with her? And why was he, Sanin, so preoccupied with these questions, he who had really nothing to do either with Polozov or his wife? Why could he not drive away that haunting image even when he turned with all his heart and soul to another one, to one who was so bright and beautiful? How dare—through those almost divine features— *these* obtrude themselves before his mind's eye? And they not only obtruded themselves—they grinned at him insolently. Those grey, predatory eyes, those dimples, those serpent-like plaits, could it be that it had all really stuck to him and that he was no longer able, that he had not the power, to shake it off, to fling it away?

Nonsense! Nonsense! Tomorrow it would all disappear without a trace. . . . But would she let him go tomorrow?

Yes. . . . He put all those questions to himself, but

when it was getting near three o'clock, he put on his black frock-coat and, after a short walk in the park, set off to the Polozovs'.

*   *   *

In their drawing-room he found a secretary of the Russian Embassy, a very tall, fair-haired German, with a horsy profile and his hair parted at the back of his head (it was a new fashion just then) and—oh, wonder of wonders—whom else besides but von Dönhof, the army officer with whom he had fought a duel a few days before! He had never expected to meet him there of all places and was taken aback involuntarily, but he did exchange bows with him.

'Do you know each other?' asked Maria Nikolayevna, whom Sanin's embarrassment did not escape.

'Yes,' said Dönhof, 'I've already had the honour,' and, bending forward a little towards Maria Nikolayevna, he added in an undertone with a smile: 'The same. . . . Your fellow-countryman . . . the Russian. . . .'

'Impossible!' she cried, also in an undertone, shook a finger at him and at once began to take leave of both him and the tall secretary who, to judge by every symptom, was head over heels in love with her, for he gaped every time he looked at her.

Dönhof left at once, with courteous submissiveness, like a friend of the family who understands immediately what is expected of him; the secretary, however, insisted on staying, but Maria Nikolayevna got rid of him without any ceremony.

'Go to your royal mistress,' she said (a certain Principessa di Monaco with a quite amazing resemblance to a street walker, who happened to live in Wiesbaden just then). 'What do you want to spend your time with a plebeian like me for?'

'But, really, madam,' the luckless secretary assured her, 'all the principessas in the world . . .'

Maria Nikolayevna was pitiless, and the secretary went away, parting and all.

Maria Nikolayevna was dressed that day very much 'to her advantage', as our grandmothers used to say. She wore a pink glacé dress with sleeves *à la Fontanges*, and a big diamond in each ear. Her eyes sparkled no less than her diamonds; she seemed in an excellent mood and in good form.

She made Sanin sit beside her and began telling him about Paris, where she was planning to go in a couple of days, about how sick and tired she was of the Germans, who were stupid when trying to be clever, and inopportunely clever when they were making fools of themselves; then she asked him point-blank, as they say, *à brûle pourpoint*, whether it was true that he had fought a duel the other day for a lady with the officer who had been there a short while ago.

'How did you know that?' murmured the astonished Sanin.

'The earth is full of rumours, my dear sir. However, I know you were right, a thousand times right, and conducted yourself like a true gentleman. Tell me, was that lady your fiancée?'

Sanin frowned a little.

'There, I won't, I won't,' Maria Nikolayevna said quickly. 'You don't like it, I'm sorry, I won't! Don't be angry, please!' Polozov appeared from the next room with a sheet of newspaper in his hands. 'What's up? Or is dinner served?'

'Dinner will be served presently, but just have a look at what I've read in the *Northern Bee*. Prince Gromoboy is dead.'

Maria Nikolayevna raised her head.

'Oh well, may he rest in peace. Every year, in February, on my birthday,' she turned to Sanin, 'he used to fill all my rooms with camellias. But it was hardly worth spending the winter in Petersburg for that. He must have been over seventy, don't you think?' she asked her husband.

'Yes, he was. There's a description of his funeral in the paper. The whole court was present. There's also a poem by Prince Kovrizhkin on the occasion.'

'Well, that's splendid then!'

'Want me to read it? The Prince calls him a man of wise counsel.'

'No, thank you. A man of wise counsel indeed! He was simply Tatyana Yuryevna's husband. Let's go in to dinner. Life is for the living. Your arm, please, Monsieur Sanin!'

*　　*　　*

The dinner was, as on the day before, wonderful, and passed off very animatedly. Maria Nikolayevna knew how to tell a story—a rare gift in a woman, and especially a Russian one! She was not afraid to be outspoken; she did not spare her countrywomen in particular. Sanin had to burst out laughing many times at some of her neat, pointed remarks. Most of all Maria Nikolayevna could not bear hypocrisy, high-sounding words and falsehood. . . . She found hypocrisy everywhere. She seemed to enjoy boasting of the low social environment in which her life began; she told rather strange stories of the relations she had known as a young girl; she described herself as an ordinary peasant woman, no worse than Natalya Kirilovna Naryshkin. It was clear to Sanin that she must have been through a lot more in her life than a great many women of her age.

153

Polozov meanwhile went on eating deliberately and drinking attentively, and only occasionally glanced at his wife and at Sanin with his whitish, apparently unseeing but actually very sharp-sighted eyes.

'What a clever darling you are!' cried Maria Nikolayevna, turning to him. 'How well you carried out all my commissions in Frankfort! I'd like to kiss you on your forehead for it, but then you're not very keen on my kisses, are you, my sweet?'

'Afraid not,' replied Polozov, cutting a pineapple with a silver knife.

Maria Nikolayevna looked at him and rapped on the table with her fingers.

'So our bet's on, isn't it?' she said significantly.

'It's on.'

'All right. You'll lose it.'

Polozov thrust out his chin.

'Well, this time,' he said, 'I think you're going to lose, however certain you may be you'll win.'

'What's the bet about? May I know?' asked Sanin.

'No, I'm afraid not now,' replied Maria Nikolayevna, and laughed.

It struck seven. The waiter announced that the carriage was waiting. Polozov saw his wife off and at once shambled back to his chair.

'Mind, don't forget the letter to my agent,' Maria Nikolayevna called after him from the hall.

'I'll write. Don't worry. I always do what I promise.'

IN 1840 the theatre in Wiesbaden was, even externally,
a sorry sight, and for pompous and pitiful mediocrity,
for painstaking and vulgar routine, its company was
not by a hair's breadth above the level which even today can be considered as normal in all German theatres
and which has been shown up to perfection by the
Karlsruhe company under the 'distinguished' direction of Herr Devrient. Behind the box, taken for 'Her
Serenity Madame von Polozov' (goodness only knows
how the waiter managed to get it—unless he really did
bribe the Stadt-Direktor!), behind the box was a small
room with sofas all along its walls; before she went in
Maria Nikolayevna asked Sanin to draw the curtains
which shut the box off from the auditorium.

'I don't want to be seen,' she said, 'or else they'll be
coming in here.'

She made him, too, sit down beside her with his back
to the auditorium so that the box should appear to be
empty.

The orchestra played the overture from *The Marriage of Figaro*. . . . The curtain went up: the play
began.

It was one of those numerous home-made works in
which well-read but third-rate authors, in choice but

colourless language, diligently but clumsily advance some 'profound' or 'vital' idea, present a so-called tragic conflict, and bore everybody to death. Maria Nikolayevna listened patiently to half of an act, but when the *jeune premier*, learning of the betrayal of his beloved (he was dressed in a brown suit with 'puffs' and a velveteen collar, a striped waistcoat with mother-of-pearl buttons, green breeches with straps of patent leather and white chamois-leather gloves), when this lover pressed both his fists to his breast, stuck out his elbows at a sharp angle, and started howling absolutely like a dog, Maria Nikolayevna could stand it no longer.

'The worst kind of French actor in the worst kind of provincial town acts better and more naturally than the most famous German celebrity,' she cried with indignation, getting up and sitting down in the little back room. 'Come here,' she said to Sanin, patting the sofa beside her. 'Let's talk.'

Sanin obeyed.

Maria Nikolayevna glanced at him.

'I can see you're one of those who do as they're told! Your wife will find you easy to get on with. That clown,' she went on, pointing with the end of her fan to the howling actor (he was acting the part of a tutor), 'reminded me of the time when I was a young girl: I, too, was in love with a teacher. It was my first—no, my second—love affair. The first time I fell in love with a novice of a Don monastery. I was twelve. I only saw him on Sundays. He wore a velvet cassock, smelt of lavender water and as he pushed through the crowd with a censer, used to say to the ladies in French: "*Pardon, excusez*"—and never raised his eyes, and he had eyelashes like that!' Maria Nikolayevna marked off with the nail of her thumb more than half of her little finger and showed it to Sanin. 'My teacher was called—Monsieur Gaston! I must tell you he was a terribly learned person and a great disciplinarian. He was Swiss and he had such an energetic face! Side-whiskers as black as pitch, a Greek profile, and lips like cast iron! I was terrified of him. He was the only man I've ever been afraid of in all my life. He was my brother's tutor. My brother died afterwards—was drowned: a gipsy woman told me that I, too, would die a violent death, but that's nonsense. I don't believe in things like that. Can you imagine my husband with a dagger?'

'Why a dagger?' remarked Sanin. 'There are other ways of dying.'

'It's all nonsense! You're not superstitious, are you? I'm not. Not a bit. And what is to be, will be. Monsieur Gaston lived in our house, in the room above me. I used to wake up at night and hear his footsteps —he went to bed very late—and my heart would stand still with veneration, or some other feeling. My father was practically illiterate himself, but he gave us an excellent education. Do you know that I can understand Latin?'

'You? Latin?'

'Yes—me! Monsieur Gaston taught me. I read the *Aeneid* with him. It's a dull thing, but there are fine passages in it. You remember when Dido and Aeneas are in the wood . . .'

'Yes, yes, I remember,' Sanin said hastily. He had long ago forgotten his Latin and had only a vague idea of the *Aeneid*.

Maria Nikolayevna glanced at him, as was her habit, a little sideways and upwards.

'Don't think, though, that I'm very learned. . . . Good heavens, no! I'm no scholar and I have no talents of any kind. I can hardly write—seriously! Can't read

anything aloud, nor play the piano, nor draw, nor sew
—nothing! That's what I'm like—that's me all over!'

She spread out her hands helplessly.

'I'm telling you all this,' she went on, 'first of all,
because I don't want to listen to those fools' (she
pointed to the stage where, at that moment, an actress,
instead of the actor, was howling, with her elbows stuck
out in front of her), 'and, secondly, because I'm in
your debt: you told me all about yourself yesterday.'

'You asked me to,' observed Sanin.

Maria Nikolayevna suddenly turned to him.

'But don't you want to know what sort of woman I
really am? I'm not surprised, though,' she added, again
leaning back on the cushions of the sofa. 'A man is
about to get married, and for love, too, *and* after a
duel. . . . Why should he bother to think of anything
else?'

Maria Nikolayevna sank into thought and began
biting the handle of her fan with her large, but even,
milk-white teeth.

And Sanin felt rising to his head again the obsession
he had not been able to get rid of for the last two
days.

The conversation between him and Maria Nikolayevna went on in an undertone, almost in a whisper,
and this irritated and excited him even more. . . .

When would it all end?

Weak people never put an end to anything themselves: they always expect things to come to an end.

On the stage someone was sneezing; the sneezing
had been introduced by the author as a comic relief or
'element'; there was, needless to say, no other comic
element in it; the spectators, pleased with this comic
relief, laughed.

That laughter, too, irritated Sanin.

There were moments when he simply did not know whether he was angry or glad, bored or enjoying himself. Oh, if Gemma could have seen him!

*　　*　　*

'It really is strange,' Maria Nikolayevna began suddenly. 'A man tells you and in such a calm voice, too: "I'm going to get married," but no one tells you calmly: "I'm going to throw myself into the river." And yet what difference is there? Strange!'

Sanin felt vexed.

'There's a great difference! Someone may not find throwing himself into a river so very terrible: he may be able to swim. Moreover, as to the strangeness of marriages—I mean, well—if that's what you find so strange, then——'

He fell silent suddenly and bit his tongue.

Maria Nikolayevna struck her hand with her fan.

'Finish what you were going to say, my dear sir, finish what you were going to say. I know what it was: "If that's what you find so strange, my dear Mrs. Polozov," you were going to say, "anything stranger than *your* marriage one could hardly imagine. . . . You see, I've known your husband since he was a little boy!" That's what you were going to say, you who can swim.'

'Please,' began Sanin.

'Isn't it true? Isn't it?' Maria Nikolayevna said insistently. 'Look me in the face and tell me that it isn't true!'

Sanin did not know where to look. . . .

'Very well,' he said at last, 'if you must know, it is true!'

Maria Nikolayevna nodded.

'Yes—yes. Well, and didn't you ask yourself, you

159

who can swim, what could be the reason for such a strange action on the part of a woman who is neither poor, nor stupid, nor bad-looking? This may not interest you, but never mind, I'll tell you the reason, not now, but at the end of the intermission. I'm always afraid that someone might come in. . . .'

Maria Nikolayevna had hardly time to finish the sentence when the outer door actually half-opened and a head was thrust into the box—a red, oily, perspiring, still young but already toothless head, with sleek long hair, a pendulous nose, enormous bat-like ears, with gold spectacles on inquisitive, dull eyes, and a pince-nez over the spectacles. . . . The head looked round, saw Maria Nikolayevna, grinned repulsively and began to nod. . . . A scraggy neck stretched out after it. . . .

Maria Nikolayevna waved it away with her handkerchief.

'I'm not at home. . . . *Ich bin nicht zu Hause, Herr P. . . .! Ich bin nicht zu Hause. . . .* Shoo! . . . Shoo! . . .'

The head looked surprised, gave a forced laugh, said, as though in a whimper, in imitation of Liszt, at whose feet it had once grovelled: '*Sehr gut! Sehr gut!*' and vanished.

'Who's the fellow?' asked Sanin.

'That one? A Wiesbaden critic. A "literary" person or a hired flunkey, whichever you prefer. He's in the pay of a local contractor and therefore must praise everything and go into raptures over everything, while he himself is full to the brim of the nastiest bile, which he dare not release. I am terrified. You see, he is a terrible scandalmonger: he'll run at once and tell everybody that I'm in the theatre. Oh, never mind!'

The orchestra played through a waltz, the curtain went up again. . . . The grimacing and whimpering began on the stage again. . . .

'Well, sir,' began Maria Nikolayevna, sitting down on the sofa again, 'since you've been trapped and are obliged to sit with me instead of enjoying the company of your fiancée—don't roll your eyes like that and don't be angry—I understand you and have already promised you—haven't I?—to let you go free, so you may as well hear my confession now. Do you want to know what I like best of all?'

'Freedom,' prompted Sanin.

Maria Nikolayevna laid her hand on his hand.

'Yes, my dear sir,' she said, and there was a peculiar note in her voice, a note of some unmistakable sincerity and gravity, 'freedom more than anything else and before everything else. And don't think I'm boasting of this—there's nothing praiseworthy about it—only it *is* so and always will *be* so with me to the end of my days. You see, I saw so much of slavery in my childhood and suffered too much from it. And, well, my teacher, Monsieur Gaston, opened my eyes, too. Now perhaps you understand why I married Ippolit: with him I'm free, absolutely as free as air, as the wind. . . . And I knew that before I married him. I knew that with him I should be a free Cossack!'

Maria Nikolayevna paused a little and flung her fan aside.

'I'll tell you one thing more: I'm quite ready to think things out. It's great fun and, after all, that's why we've been given brains, but I never think about the consequences of what I do myself, and when I do, I am never even a *tiny* bit sorry for myself; it's not worth it. I have a favourite saying: *cela ne tire pas à conséquence* —I don't know how to translate it. And, indeed, why *tire à conséquence?* You see, no one will ask me to give an account of myself *here*, on this earth—and up there' (she raised a finger aloft) '—well, up there—let them

M   161

do what they like. When they come to try me *there*, *I* shall no longer exist! Are you listening to me? You're not bored, are you?'

Sanin was sitting with his head bowed. He now raised it.

'I'm not at all bored, and I'm listening to you with interest. Only I—I must confess I can't help asking myself: why are you telling me all this?'

Maria Nikolayevna moved a little closer to him on the sofa.

'You can't help asking yourself? . . . Are you so slow in the uptake? Or so modest?'

Sanin raised his head higher than before.

'I'm telling you all this,' Maria Nikolayevna went on in a calm tone of voice, which did not, however, altogether correspond with the expression of her face, 'because I like you very much. Yes—don't be surprised, I'm not joking; because having met you I'd hate to think that you'd be left with a bad impression of me—and not so much a bad one—I shouldn't mind that—as a wrong one. That's why I've got you to come here, that's why I'm staying alone with you and talking to you so frankly. . . . Yes, yes, frankly. I'm not telling you a lie. And please remember, I know that you're in love with another woman and are going to marry her. . . . So be fair to me, for I'm entirely disinterested! Still, here's your chance to say in your turn: *cela ne tire pas à conséquence!*'

She laughed, but her laughter was cut short suddenly—and she remained motionless as though struck by her own words, and in her eyes, usually so gay and bold, there was a look of something like timidity and even sadness.

'A snake! Oh, she's a snake!' Sanin was thinking meanwhile. 'But what a beautiful snake!'

'Pass me my lorgnette, please,' Maria Nikolayevna said suddenly. 'I want to see whether that *jeune première* really is so ugly. You know, I can't help thinking that the Government must have given her her job in the interests of morality to make sure that the young men do not fall in love too easily.'

Sanin handed her the lorgnette and, as she took it from him, she swiftly, though scarcely audibly, snatched his hand in both of hers.

'Don't be so serious,' she whispered with a smile. 'You know, no one can put fetters on me, but then I don't put fetters on anyone, either. I love freedom and do not recognize any obligations—not only for myself. And now move away a little and let's listen to the play.'

Maria Nikolayevna turned her lorgnette on the stage and Sanin began looking in the same direction, sitting beside her in the semi-darkness of the box, and breathing in, involuntarily breathing in, the warmth and fragrance of her gorgeous body and as involuntarily turning over in his mind everything she had been telling him in the course of the evening—especially during the last few minutes. . . .

40

THE play went on for over an hour, but Maria Nikolayevna and Sanin soon stopped looking at the stage.
They had started a conversation again and it, the conversation, that is, went on on the same lines as before;
only this time Sanin was less silent. Inwardly he was
angry with himself and with Maria Nikolayevna; he
tried to prove to her the utter superficiality of her
'theory', as though she were interested in theories! He
began arguing with her, which she was secretly very
glad of: if he argued, then he was giving in or would be
giving in. He had taken the bait, he was yielding, he
was no longer shy of her! She raised objections, laughed,
agreed with him, pondered, attacked. . . . And meanwhile his face and her face came closer together and his
eyes no longer turned away from hers. Those eyes of
hers seemed to wander, to rove over his features, and
he smiled at her in reply—politely, but smiled. It
suited her that he should be indulging in abstractions,
arguing about the honesty of intimate relationships,
about duty, the sanctity of love and marriage. It is, indeed, a well-known fact that these abstractions come in
very useful indeed as a beginning, as a starting-point.
   People who knew Maria Nikolayevna well maintained
that when something tender and modest, something

almost virginally coy, suddenly broke through that strong and powerful personality of hers—though, come to think of it, where did it come from?—then, why, then the affair took a dangerous turn.

Apparently it had taken that turn for Sanin too. . . . He would have despised himself if he had managed to concentrate his attention for a single moment; but he did not have time either to concentrate, or to despise himself.

She wasted no time. And it all arose from his being so very good-looking! What is there left but to say: 'You never can tell when you are winning or losing!'

The play was over. Maria Nikolayevna asked Sanin to help her on with her shawl and she did not stir while he wrapped the soft material round her truly regal shoulders. Then she took his arm, went out into the corridor and—nearly screamed: at the very door of the box, like some apparition, stood Dönhof, drawn up to his full height, and from behind his back peeped out the nasty little figure of the Wiesbaden critic. The oily face of 'the man of letters' simply shone with malicious joy.

'You wouldn't like me to get your carriage, would you, madam?' the young army officer addressed Maria Nikolayevna, with a tremor of barely controlled fury in his voice.

'No, thank you,' she replied, 'my servant will get it. You're not to follow me!' she added in an imperious whisper, withdrawing rapidly and dragging Sanin after her.

'Go to hell!' Dönhof suddenly snarled at the 'man of letters'. 'What are you following me about for?'

He had to vent his fury on someone!

'*Sehr gut! Sehr gut!*' murmured the man of letters, and effaced himself.

Maria Nikolayevna's servant, who had been waiting for her in the foyer, found her carriage in less than no time. She got into it quickly and Sanin sprang in after her. The doors slammed to, and Maria Nikolayevna burst into loud laughter.

'What are you laughing at?' Sanin wanted to know.

'Oh, I'm awfully sorry, but I couldn't help thinking, what if Dönhof were to fight a duel with you again—over me? Wouldn't that be extraordinary?'

'Why, are you such very great friends with him?' asked Sanin.

'With him? With that boy? He runs errands for me. You needn't worry.'

'I'm not worried at all.'

Maria Nikolayevna sighed.

'Oh well, I know you're not. But listen: you know, you're so nice, you mustn't refuse me one last request. Don't forget I shall be leaving for Paris in three days and you will be returning to Frankfort. We shall never meet again.'

'What's your request?'

'You can ride, of course, can't you?'

'I can.'

'Well, it's this. Tomorrow morning I'll take you with me—and we'll go riding together into the country. We'll have excellent horses. Then we'll return, conclude our business and—goodbye for ever! Don't look surprised, don't tell me it's just a whim, that I'm crazy—it may be so, but just say: I agree!'

Maria Nikolayevna turned her face to him. It was dark in the carriage, but her eyes flashed in that very darkness.

'Very well, I agree,' Sanin said with a sigh.

'Oh, you sighed!' Maria Nikolayevna mimicked him. 'I suppose what you mean is: in for a penny, in

166

for a pound. . . . But no, no. . . . You're sweet, you're good, and I shall keep my promise. Here's my hand, without a glove, my right hand, my business hand. Take it and believe in the sincerity of its pressure. I don't know what sort of a woman I am, but I'm an honest business woman and one can do business with me.'

Without realizing very well what he was doing, Sanin lifted the hand to his lips. She took it away gently and fell silent suddenly, and remained silent until the carriage stopped.

She started getting out. . . . What was it? Did Sanin imagine it or did he really feel that something hot brushed swiftly against his cheek?

'Till tomorrow!' whispered Maria Nikolayevna to him on the stairs, lit up by the four candles of a candelabrum held aloft at her appearance by the gold-braided doorman. She kept her eyes lowered.

'Till tomorrow!'

On returning to his room, Sanin found on the table a letter from Gemma. He instantly felt dismayed and at once pretended to be overjoyed so as to conceal his dismay from himself.

The letter consisted of a few lines. She was delighted at the favourable 'beginning of his business', advised him to be patient, adding that all at home were well and that they were all rejoicing at the prospect of his return. Sanin found the letter rather dry—still, he took pen and paper and threw it all down again. 'Why write? I shall be back myself tomorrow—it's time, high time!'

He went to bed at once and tried to fall asleep as quickly as possible. . . . If he had not gone to bed but remained awake he would have started thinking about Gemma, and for some reason he was ashamed to think about her. His conscience pricked him. But he re-assured himself with the thought that tomorrow it would all be over for ever and that he would part for ever from that preposterous rich woman—and would forget all this idiotic nonsense!

Weak people, when communing with themselves, are fond of using vigorous expressions.

Et puis—cela ne tire pas à conséquence!

41

THAT was what Sanin thought as he went to bed; but what he thought next morning when Maria Niko-layevna knocked impatiently at his door with the coral handle of her riding-whip, when he saw her on the threshold of his room with the train of a dark-blue riding–habit over her arm, with a man's small hat on her thickly plaited hair, with a veil thrown over her shoulder, with a smile of invitation on her lips, in her eyes and over all her face—what he thought then—history is silent about.

'Well, are you ready?' her gay voice rang out.

Sanin buttoned his coat and silently picked up his hat.

Maria Nikolayevna threw a bright look at him, nodded and ran quickly down the stairs. And he ran after her.

The horses were already waiting in the street, at the front steps. There were three of them: a golden chestnut, thoroughbred mare with a thin-skinned muzzle that showed her teeth, prominent black eyes, stag's legs, a little lean and muscular, but beautiful and fiery—for Maria Nikolayevna; a big, powerful, rather heavily built horse, raven black all over—for Sanin; the third horse was for the groom. Maria Nikolayevna leapt adroitly on to her mare. . . . The mare stamped and wheeled round, raising her tail and sinking on her haunches, but Maria Nikolayevna (an excellent horsewoman!) reined her in. They had to say goodbye to Polozov, who appeared on the balcony in his inevitable fez and in a wide-open dressing-gown, and was waving from there with his cambric handker-chief; he was not smiling, though, but rather frowning. Sanin, too, mounted his horse; Maria Nikolayevna saluted Polozov with her riding-whip, then struck her mare with it on her arched and broad neck; the mare reared, leapt forward and moved with a smart, shor-tened step, quivering in every sinew, chewing the bit, biting the air and snorting abruptly. Sanin rode behind and looked at Maria Nikolayevna—her slender, supple figure, in a close-fitting though not too tight corset, swayed confidently, gracefully and skilfully. She turned back her head and beckoned to him with her eyes alone. He came alongside.

'You see how wonderful it is,' she said. 'I'm telling you for the last time before we part—you are sweet and you won't regret it.'

Having uttered these last words, she nodded her head several times as though wishing to confirm them and make him realize their significance.

She looked so happy that Sanin was simply amazed: there even appeared on her face that demure expression which children assume when they are very, very pleased.

They rode up to the nearby tollgate at a walking pace and after that rode off at a quick trot along the highroad. The weather was glorious, real summer weather: the wind blew gently in their faces and rang and whistled pleasantly in their ears. They felt happy: both were overwhelmed by a sense of youth and robust health and free, impetuous onward motion; it grew stronger every moment.

Maria Nikolayevna reined in her horse again and again rode on at a walking pace; Sanin followed her example.

'This,' she began with a deep, blissful sigh, 'this makes life worth living. If you succeed in doing what you want and what seemed impossible, then you jolly well make full use of it, enjoy it to the full!' She passed her hand across her throat. 'And how good you feel yourself then! Now, for instance, I—I feel such a good person! I feel like flinging my arms round the whole world. That is, no—not the *whole* world! That one,' she indicated with her riding-whip a poorly clad old man who was walking along the edge of the road, 'that one I wouldn't have embraced. But I'm ready to make him happy. Here, take this,' she cried loudly in German, and threw her purse at his feet.

The heavy little bag (there were no leather purses in those days) fell with a thud on to the roadway. The passer-by stopped in surprise, but Maria Nikolayevna burst out laughing and went off at a gallop.

'Do you enjoy riding so much?' asked Sanin, overtaking her.

Maria Nikolayevna again reined in her horse: she did not stop it otherwise.

'I only wanted to get away from his thanks. He who thanks me, kills my pleasure. You see, I didn't do it for him. I did it for myself. How dare he thank me in that case? I'm sorry. I didn't catch your question.'

'I asked—I wanted to know why you are so gay today?'

'You know,' said Maria Nikolayevna (she had either not heard Sanin's question again or did not think it necessary to answer it), 'I'm awfully sick of that groom who keeps following us and, I suppose, wondering when the lady and the gentleman will be going home. How are we to get rid of him?' She quickly got a little notebook out of her pocket, 'Send him back to town with a note? No—that won't do. Ah, I've got it! What's that in front of us? An inn?'

Sanin looked in the direction she pointed.

'Yes, I believe it is.'

'Well, that's excellent. I'll tell him to stay at that inn and drink beer till we return.'

'But what will he think?'

'What do we care? Anyway, he won't think anything. He'll drink beer—that's all. Well, Sanin' (she called him for the first time by his surname only), 'forward at a gallop!'

When they reached the inn, Maria Nikolayevna called the groom up and told him what she wanted him to do. The groom, a man of English extraction and English temperament, raised his hand to the peak of his cap without a word, jumped off the horse and took it by the bridle.

'Well, now we're as free as birds!' cried Maria Nikolayevna. 'Where shall we go? North, south, east or west? Look, I'm like the King of Hungary at his coronation' (she pointed her whip to the four corners of the world). 'Everything's ours! No, do you know what? See those glorious mountains there—and that wonderful forest! Let's go there! To the mountains, to the mountains!

'*In die Berge, wo die Freiheit thront.*'

She turned off the highroad and galloped off along a narrow untrodden track, which really seemed to lead to the mountains. Sanin galloped after her.

42

THIS track soon changed into a narrow footpath and at last completely disappeared, cut across by a ditch. Sanin thought they had better go back, but Maria Nikolayevna said: 'No! I want to get to the mountains! Let's ride straight on as the crow flies,' and made her horse jump over the ditch. Sanin, too, jumped over it. Beyond the ditch was a meadow, dry at first, then wet, and farther on quite swampy: the water oozed out of the ground everywhere and here and there stood in pools. Maria Nikolayevna let her horse go straight through those pools on purpose, laughing and saying again and again: 'Let's be schoolchildren again!'

'Do you know,' she asked Sanin, 'the meaning of thaw-hunting?'

'I know.'

'My uncle was a huntsman,' she went on. 'I used to go hunting with him—in the spring. Oh, it was wonderful! So you and I, too, are now "thaw-hunting". The only thing I object to is that a Russian like you should be marrying an Italian girl. However, that's your funeral. What's this? Another ditch? Over!'

The horse jumped over, but Maria Nikolayevna's hat fell off and her hair tumbled all over her shoulders. Sanin was about to dismount and pick up her hat, but she shouted to him: 'Don't touch it! I'll pick it up myself,' and bending low over the saddle, caught hold of the veil with the handle of her riding-whip and, to be sure, picked up her hat, put it on, but did not do up her hair and galloped off again and even uttered a whoop of delight. Sanin galloped along beside her, leapt over ditches, fences, streams, fell in and scrambled out, dashed downhill, dashed uphill and kept looking at her face. What a face it was! It seemed all wide-open: wide-open eyes—bright and wild and rapacious; lips, nostrils also wide-open and breathing greedily; she looked straight ahead, and it seemed as if that soul wanted to take possession of everything it saw—the earth, the sky, the sun and the air itself, and that it regretted one thing only: that there were too few dangers—it would have liked to overcome them all! 'Sanin,' she shouted, 'why, this is like Bürger's *Lenore*! Only you're not dead, are you? Not dead? . . . I'm alive!' Her powerful body responded to the call of the blood. It was no longer an Amazon urging her horse on to a gallop, it was a young female Centaur—half beast, half god—galloping at full speed, and the sedate, civilized countryside is amazed as it is trampled underfoot in her wild riot.

Maria Nikolayevna at last drew up her foaming and

173

mud-bespattered horse, which was staggering under her, while Sanin's powerful but heavy stallion was gasping for breath.

'Well, like it?' asked Maria Nikolayevna in a sort of wonderful whisper.

'I do!' Sanin replied ecstatically.

His blood, too, was on fire.

'Wait, this isn't all!' she said, holding out her hand.

The glove on her hand was torn across.

'I promised to bring you to the woods and the mountains. Well, there they are—the mountains!'

And, indeed, within two hundred yards of the place where the high-spirited riders had stopped in their wild career, rose the mountains, covered with tall trees.

'Look, here's the road. Let's carry on. Only slowly. We must let our horses get their breath.'

They rode off. Maria Nikolayevna tossed back her hair with one powerful sweep of her hand. Then she glanced at her gloves and took them off.

'My hands will smell of leather,' she said. 'You don't mind, do you?'

Maria Nikolayevna smiled and Sanin, too, smiled. That wild gallop of theirs seemed to have finally brought them together and made them friends.

'How old are you?' she asked suddenly.

'Twenty-two.'

'No? I'm also twenty-two. It's a nice age. Add them together and it's still a long way to old age. It's hot, though. Am I very red in the face?'

'Red as a poppy!'

Maria Nikolayevna wiped her face with a handkerchief.

'Let's first get to the forest, it will be cool there. It's such an old forest, just like an old friend. Have you any friends?'

Sanin thought for a moment.

'Yes, I have. Only not very many. No real ones.'

'Well, I have real ones—only not old ones. Here's another of my friends—my horse. How carefully she carries you! Oh, but it's lovely here! Am I really going off to Paris the day after tomorrow?'

'Are you?' Sanin asked with a note of regret in his voice.

'And you to Frankfort?'

'Why, yes. Most certainly.'

'Well, good luck! But today is ours—ours—ours!'

*　　*　　*

The horses reached the edge of the forest and rode into it. The shade of the forest covered them on all sides, wide and soft.

'Why,' cried Maria Nikolayevna, 'it's heavenly here! Let's go farther, deeper into the shade, Sanin!'

The horses moved slowly on, 'deeper into the shade', swaying gently and snorting. The path, along which they were riding, suddenly turned off and plunged into a rather narrow gorge. The smell of heather, bracken, pine-resin and last year's decaying leaves, heavy and drowsy, hung in the air. Strong currents of fresh air came from the clefts in the big, brown rocks. On either side of the path rose round mounds covered with green moss.

'Stop!' cried Maria Nikolayevna, 'I want to sit down and rest on this velvet. Help me to dismount.'

Sanin jumped off his horse and ran up to her. She leaned on his shoulders, leapt instantly to the ground and sat down on one of the mossy mounds. He stood before her, holding the reins of the two horses in his hands.

She raised her eyes to him. . . .

175

'Sanin, do you know how to forget?'

Sanin recalled what had happened the day before, in the carriage.

'What is it—a question or a reproach?'

'I've never in my life reproached anyone for anything. And do you believe in love potions?'

'In what?'

'In love potions. You know, they sing about it in our folk-songs. In our Russian peasant songs.'

'Oh, I see what you mean,' Sanin observed in a drawn-out voice.

'Yes, that's what I mean. I believe in it and you, too, will believe in it.'

'Love potions—witchcraft,' Sanin repeated. 'Anything is possible in this world. Before I didn't believe in it, but now I do. I can hardly recognize myself.'

Maria Nikolayevna thought for a moment and looked round.

'I can't help feeling,' she murmured, 'that I know this place. Have a look, Sanin. Is there a red wooden cross behind that large oak-tree? Is there?'

Sanin took a few steps to one side.

'There is.'

Maria Nikolayevna gave a self-satisfied smile.

'Ah, that's splendid! I know where we are. We haven't yet lost our way. What's that tapping? A wood-cutter?'

Sanin looked into the thicket.

'Yes, there's a man there cutting down dry branches.'

'Must tidy up my hair,' said Maria Nikolayevna. 'He might see me like this and think goodness knows what.'

She took off her hat and began plaiting up her long hair, gravely and in silence. Sanin stood before her. . . . Her shapely lines showed clearly under the dark folds of her dress with bits of moss adhering to it here and there.

One of the horses suddenly shook itself behind Sanin's back, and he himself shook all over involuntarily. Everything in him was in confusion, his nerves were stretched tight like strings on a musical instrument. It was with good reason that he had said that he did not recognize himself. He was, indeed, bewitched. . . . His entire being was full of only one desire, one thought. Maria Nikolayevna cast a searching glance at him.

'Well,' she said, putting on her hat, 'now everything's in order. Won't you sit down? Here! No, wait —don't sit down. What's this?'

A dull rumbling noise rolled over the tree-tops and through the air of the forest.

'It wouldn't be thunder, would it?'

'I think it is,' replied Sanin.

'Why, that's wonderful, simply wonderful! That was the only thing wanting!' The dull rumbling resounded once more, rose and fell—in a crash. 'Bravo! Encore! Do you remember me telling you yesterday about the *Aeneid*? *They* too were overtaken by a thunderstorm in a forest. However, we'd better be going.' She rose quickly to her feet. 'Bring my horse. Let me lean on your arm. So, I'm not heavy.'

She pulled herself into the saddle without the slightest effort. Sanin, too, mounted his horse.

'Are you going home?' he asked in an unsteady voice.

'Home!!' she replied with deliberation, taking up the reins. 'Follow me,' she ordered him almost rudely.

She rode out on to the road and, passing the red cross, rode down into a hollow, reached the turning, then turned to the right, and up another mountain path. . . . She obviously knew where the path led, and the path led deeper and deeper into the forest. She uttered no word, nor did she turn round to look at him; she rode on imperiously and he followed her meekly and obediently, without a spark of will-power in his sinking heart. It began to drizzle. She quickened the pace of her horse and he did not lag behind her. At last he caught sight of a lowly gamekeeper's hut with a low door in its wattle wall through the dark greenery of pine bushes and under an overhanging grey crag. Maria Nikolayevna made her mare push through the bushes, jumped off her and, finding herself suddenly at the entrance to the hut, turned round to Sanin and whispered 'Aeneas?'

* * *

Four hours later Maria Nikolayevna and Sanin, accompanied by the groom, who was dozing in the saddle, returned to their hotel in Wiesbaden. Polozov met his wife with the letter to the agent in his hand. Looking more closely at her, however, he showed distinct signs of displeasure on his face and even muttered:

'I haven't lost my bet, have I?'

Maria Nikolayevna merely shrugged her shoulders.

* * *

The same day, two hours later, Sanin was standing in his room before her like one beside himself and utterly ruined. . . .

'Where are you going, darling?' she asked him. 'To Paris or to Frankfort?'

'I'm going where you will be,' he replied in despair, 'and I'll be with you till you drive me away,' and he pressed his lips to the hands of his mistress. She freed them and laid them on his head, grasping his hair with

178

all her ten fingers. She slowly fingered and twisted his unresisting hair, drew herself up to her full height, her lips curled with triumph and her eyes, wide and bright, almost white, merely expressed the ruthless insensitivity and the satiety of conquest. A hawk, holding a captured bird in its claws, has eyes like that.

43

THIS was what Dimitry Sanin remembered when he found the garnet cross among his old papers in the stillness of his study. The events related by us rose clearly and consecutively before his mind's eye.... But having reached the moment when he had addressed Madame Polozov with so humiliating a supplication, when he had grovelled at her feet, when his slavery had begun —he turned away from the images he had conjured up: he did not want to recall any more. And it was not as though his memory had failed him. Oh, no! He knew, he knew very well what had followed after that moment, but he was overwhelmed by shame, even now, so many years after; he was afraid of the irresistible feeling of contempt for himself which—he had no doubt whatever about it—would sweep over him and, like a torrent, submerge all his other feelings the moment he did not bid his memory be still. But however much he tried to turn away from those memories, he could not suppress them entirely. He remembered the wretched, tearful, lying, shabby letter he had sent to Gemma, a letter that remained unanswered. . . . To go back, to return to her after such deceit, after such a betrayal—no! no! He still had that much honesty and conscience left in him. Besides, he had lost all confidence, all respect for himself: he could no longer answer for anything. Sanin also remembered how afterwards—oh, the shame of it!—he had sent Polozov's footman for his things in Frankfort, how scared he had been, how he had thought of one thing only: to leave quickly for Paris, for Paris; how, at Maria Nikolayevna's behest, he had ingratiated himself with her husband, how he had humoured him, and how he had exchanged courtesies with Dönhof, on whose finger he noticed exactly the same kind of iron ring as the one Maria Nikolayevna had given him!!! Then more memories followed, memories that were still worse and more shameful. . . . The waiter brought him a visiting-card and on it he read, 'Pantaleone Cippatola, court singer to H.H. the Duke of Modena'. He hid himself away from the old man, but could not avoid a meeting with him in the corridor, and before his mind's eye there arose the old man's furious face under the towering quiff of grey hair; the aged eyes blazed like red-hot coals, and he could hear again the menacing exclamations and curses: *Maledizione!* He could even make out the words: *Codardo! Infame traditore!*

Sanin screwed up his eyes, shook his head and turned away again and again—but he could still see himself sitting on the narrow front seat of a stage-coach. . . .

Maria Nikolayevna and Polozov occupied the comfortable back seats, and the four horses were trotting merrily along the main Wiesbaden street on the way to Paris! To Paris! Polozov was eating the pear which he, Sanin, had peeled for him, and Maria Nikolayevna was looking at him and smiling the smile he—a man already enslaved—knew so well—the smile of a proprietor, of a sovereign.

But, good Lord! There, at the corner of the street, not far from the outskirts of the town, was it not Pantaleone standing there—yes, it was Pantaleone, and who was it with him? Not Emilio? Yes, it was Emilio, the devoted, enthusiastic boy! It was not so long since that his youthful heart had been full of veneration for his hero, his ideal, but now his pale, beautiful—so beautiful that Maria Nikolayevna noticed it and put her head out of the carriage window—his noble face was now ablaze with fury and contempt; his eyes—so like *those* eyes!—were riveted on Sanin and his lips were compressed and, suddenly, they opened, but only to utter an imprecation. . . .

And Pantaleone stretched out his hand and pointed out Sanin—to whom?—to Tartaglia, who was standing beside him, and Tartaglia barked at Sanin—and the barking of that faithful dog sounded like an unbearable affront. . . . Monstrous!

And then—his life in Paris, and all the humiliations, all the hideous tortures of the slave who is not allowed to be jealous or to complain and who in the end is cast aside like a worn-out garment. . . .

Then—his return home, the poisoned, ravaged life, petty troubles, petty worries, bitter and futile regrets, and oblivion as bitter and futile, a punishment concealed from view and yet felt constantly, every minute, like some trivial but incurable pain, like the repayment

181

penny by penny of a debt the amount of which can never be calculated.

The cup was full to the brim—enough!

*　　　*　　　*

How did it happen that the little cross which Gemma had given to Sanin had been preserved, why had he not returned it? And how was it he had never come across it till that day? He sat for a long, long time deep in thought and—taught by his experience of so many years—was still quite at a loss to understand how he could have abandoned Gemma, with whom he was so tenderly and so passionately in love, for a woman whom he did not love at all. . . . Next day he surprised all his friends and acquaintances by the announcement that he was going abroad.

His decision caused general bewilderment in society. Sanin was leaving Petersburg in midwinter, having just rented and furnished an excellent flat and even taken out a season ticket for the Italian opera in which Patti herself was to take part—yes, Patti herself! His friends and acquaintances were puzzled; but people are not, as a rule, interested in somebody else's affairs for long, and when Sanin left for abroad, only his French tailor came to see him off at the railway station and that, too, in the hope of being paid in full for an outstanding account *'pour un saute-en-barque en velours noir, tout à fait chic'*.

44

SANIN told his friends that he was going abroad, but he did not tell them where: my readers will, no doubt, have guessed that he went straight to Frankfort. Thanks to the general extension of railway communications, he was there on the fourth day after leaving Petersburg. He had not visited the city since 1840. The hotel, the White Swan, was still in its old place and was still flourishing, though it was no longer considered first class. The Zeile, the principal street of Frankfort, had changed little, but there was not a trace left not only of Signora Roselli's house, but of the very street where her shop was. Sanin walked, like one distracted, about the places he had known so well, and could recognize nothing: the old buildings had disappeared; in their place were new streets of huge solid blocks of houses and elegant villas; even the public gardens, where his last meeting with Gemma had taken place, had expanded and changed to much that Sanin could not help asking himself if they really were the same gardens. What was he to do? Where and how was he to make inquiries? Thirty years had passed since then. ... It was not an easy thing. He asked all sorts of people, but they had not even heard of the name Roselli. The owner of the hotel advised him to inquire at the public

183

library where, he thought, he might find all the old newspapers, but what useful purpose that would serve, he could not say himself. In despair, Sanin asked whether he knew a certain Herr Klüber. The name was very familiar to the hotel-keeper, but there, too, nothing came of it. The elegant shop manager, having made a name for himself and risen to the status of a capitalist, ran into debt, was made bankrupt and died in prison. . . . This piece of news, though, did not cause the least bit of distress to Sanin. He was already beginning to wonder whether his journey abroad had not been rather ill-advised. . . . But one day, as he was looking through the Frankfort address book, he came across the name of von Dönhof, retired Major (*Major a.D.*). He at once took a cab and went to see him, though why that particular Dönhof should be *the* Dönhof and why even *the* Dönhof could give him any news of the Roselli family he could not say. Anyway, a drowning man clutches at a straw.

Sanin found the retired Major von Dönhof at home, and in the grey-haired gentleman who received him he at once recognized his former adversary. Dönhof, too, recognized him and was even glad to see him: it reminded him of the days of his youth and of his youthful escapades. Sanin learnt from him that the Roselli family had long ago emigrated to America and had settled in New York; that Gemma had married an American business man; that he, Dönhof, had an acquaintance, also a business man, who probably knew her husband's address, as he did a great deal of business with America. Sanin persuaded Dönhof to go and see his acquaintance and —oh, what joy! —Dönhof brought him the address of Gemma's husband, Mr. Jeremiah Slocum, 501 Broadway, New York. Only this address dated from the year 1863.

'Let's hope,' cried Dönhof, 'that our former belle of Frankfort is still alive and has not left New York. By the way,' he added, lowering his voice, 'what about that Russian lady who, you remember, was staying in Wiesbaden at that time—Madame von Bo—von Bosoloff—is she still living?'

'No,' replied Sanin, 'she died long ago.'

Dönhof raised his eyes but, noticing that Sanin had turned away and was frowning, did not add another word and took his leave.

*   *   *

The same day Sanin sent a letter to Mrs. Gemma Slocum in New York. In the letter he told her that he was writing to her from Frankfort where he had come for the sole purpose of tracing her whereabouts; that he knew perfectly well that he had not the slightest right to expect a reply from her; that he did not deserve her forgiveness in any way and only hoped that she had long forgotten his very existence among the happy surroundings in which she lived. He added that he had taken the liberty of reminding her of himself as a result of a chance circumstance which had aroused in him vivid memories of his past; he told her about his own lonely and unhappy bachelor life; he conjured her to understand the reasons which had induced him to write to her—not to let him carry to the grave the bitter sense of his guilt, a guilt he had long atoned for by suffering, but for which he had not yet obtained forgiveness, and to make him happy with the briefest news of her life in the new world to which she had gone. 'In writing just one word to me,' Sanin concluded his letter, 'you will be performing a good deed worthy of your noble soul, and I shall thank you to my last breath. I am staying here at the *White Swan*' (he underlined these words) 'and shall wait, wait till spring, for your answer.'

He posted this letter and waited for a reply. He spent six weeks at the hotel, scarcely leaving his room and seeing absolutely no one. No one could write to him from Russia or from anywhere else; and he was glad of that; for if a letter addressed to him did come, he would know at once that it was the one he was waiting for. He read from morning till night, not newspapers but serious books, historical works. These continuous readings, this stillness around him, this snail-like, secluded existence—all this seemed to agree perfectly with his mood: he felt grateful to Gemma for this alone! But was she alive? Would she reply?

At last a letter addressed to him arrived with an American postmark, from New York. The handwriting of the address on the envelope was English. He did not recognize it and his heart sank. . . . It was some time before he could make up his mind to open the letter. He glanced at the signature: Gemma! Tears started to his eyes: the very fact that she signed the letter by her Christian name was already a pledge of reconciliation, of forgiveness! He unfolded the thin sheet of blue notepaper and a photograph dropped out of it. He picked it up quickly and was struck dumb with amazement: Gemma, the living image of Gemma as he had known her thirty years ago! The same eyes, the same lips, the same cast of countenance. On the back of the photograph was written: 'My daughter Marianne.' The whole letter was simple and very affectionate. Gemma thanked Sanin for not having hesitated to write to her, for having shown confidence in her; she did not conceal from him the fact that after his flight she had indeed gone through some painful

186

moments, but added at once that in spite of that she considered—had always considered—that she was very fortunate in meeting him, for that meeting had prevented her from becoming the wife of Herr Klüber and that in that way he, Sanin, was responsible, however indirectly, for her marriage to her present husband with whom she had been living for twenty-eight years very happily, in comfort and prosperity: their house was known to everybody in New York. Gemma informed Sanin that she had five children, four sons and one eighteen-year-old daughter, who was already engaged to be married and whose photograph she was sending him because she was generally considered to be very like her mother. Her sad news Gemma kept to the end of her letter. Frau Lenore had died in New York, where she had followed her daughter and her son-in-law, but she had lived long enough to rejoice in the happiness of her children and nurse her grandchildren; Pantaleone had also been planning to go to America, but he had died on the very eve of his departure from Frankfort. 'And Emilio, our darling, our incomparable Emilio, died a glorious death for the freedom of his country, in Sicily, where he had gone as one of the "Thousand" under the leadership of the great Garibaldi. We all deeply mourned the death of our beloved brother, but even while shedding tears we were proud of him and we shall always be proud of him and hold his memory sacred! His great, selfless soul was worthy of a martyr's crown!' Then Gemma expressed her regret that Sanin's life had apparently turned out so badly and wished him, above all, peace of mind and calmness of spirit, saying in conclusion that she would have been glad to see him, though she realized how very unlikely such a meeting was. . . .

We will not attempt to describe the feelings Sanin

experienced when reading this letter. There is no satisfactory expression for such feelings: they are too deep
and strong and far too elusive for any word. Only
music could express them.

Sanin answered at once, and as a wedding present to
the bride, he sent 'Marianne Slocum from an unknown
friend' the garnet cross, set in a magnificent pearl
necklace. This present, expensive though it was, did
not ruin him: during the thirty years which had passed
since his first visit to Frankfort he had managed to
amass a considerable fortune. He returned to Petersburg at the beginning of May, but apparently not for
long. It is rumoured that he is selling his estates and is
about to leave for America.

Baden-Baden. 1871

Printed in the USA
CPSIA information can be obtained
at www.ICGtesting.com
LVHW091133150724
785511LV00001B/117

9 780374 526627